THE GOSPEL OF US

For the teachers and listeners

Owen Sheers

The
Gospel
of
Us

SEREN

Seren is the book imprint of
Poetry Wales Press Ltd
57 Nolton Street, Bridgend, Wales, CF31 3AE
www.serenbooks.com

ISBN 978-1-85411- 622-2

Front cover design: Dave McKean www.mckean-art.co.uk
Back cover photograph: Owen Sheers www.owensheers.co.uk
Inner design and typesetting by books@lloydrobson.com

Printed by Bell and Bain, Glasgow

The Gospel of Us was first commissioned and published by National Theatre
Wales as part of its production of *The Passion*, produced with Wildworks in
Port Talbot in April 2011.

The publisher acknowledges the financial support of
the Welsh Books Council.

Foreword

It began with an actor, a producer and a poet sitting in a room talking about the seed of an idea. The actor was Michael Sheen, the producer was Lucy Davies of National Theatre Wales and I was the poet. NTW was planning its first year of site-specific productions. An ambitious schedule of a new production every month, all over Wales, hardly any performed in a theatre. Lucy had approached Michael to ask him what, if he were given the opportunity of working with this new national company, would he like to do? Michael told her he'd like to go back to Port Talbot, his hometown, and create a piece of contemporary theatre in response to the community Passion plays he'd once seen there as a teenager. It was at this point Lucy approached me about writing the script. She'd read a few lines in one of my poems which seemed to echo a note of Michael's idea, and she thought perhaps that might be true of the project as a whole too; that a poet, rather than a conventional playwright, might suit the nature of the production.

'It's not matter that matters,
or our thoughts and words
but the shadows they throw
against the lives of others.'

From *Shadow Man*

At the time of that first meeting none of us knew what *The Passion* would be. We didn't even know it would be called *The Passion*. What we did know, however, was *where* it would be, so that's where we went next.

Like most people in South Wales I knew Port Talbot more as a view than a place, its constellation-lit steelworks a strangely seductive manifestation of Blake's 'dark satanic mills'. I'd seen those steelworks as, like hundreds of thousands of others, I'd driven along the stretch of M4 motorway that rises above the town. On the day of our visit, however, for the first time I walked through the town instead, guided by Michael and his memories of growing up there. With Lucy we walked along the front and down onto a slipway where we looked out at a saturation of sea disappearing towards a distant horizon. We walked along the wind-harried beach, tyre tracks coiling like ammonite fossils in the sand. We wandered between the graffitied pillars that support the M4 above a space of ground where a terrace of houses once stood. We went into a school, the shopping centre, a club. We stood in the middle of a roundabout and imagined a cross. And all the time we talked, so that by the time we left Port Talbot later that evening *The Passion*, a site-specific play performed over three days in Easter 2011, was already taking shape.

The final script and performance of *The Passion* was as much a response to Port Talbot as it was a response to the Christian tradition of the Passion plays once performed there. It was a piece of theatre grown from a conversation with the town and its people. As we neared the performance date, however, we realised the play wouldn't only be a result of that conversation, but would be continuing it too; in many guises, across many different forms. It already existed as a rumour in the town. Other people were becoming aware of it online, and would go on to follow the unfolding narrative via a website, Twitter and Facebook. The performance would be filmed, as a documentary, as a feature film and on thousands of personal cameras and phones. Like the gospels upon which the original Passion plays were based, the perspectives of witness were to be multiple.

It was within this varied narrative environment that Lucy asked me to write a synopsis of the play's action, so an audience member who only caught some of the three-day performance might catch up with what had happened so far. In any other instance I may have written just that: a synopsis of plot and story. But somehow that didn't seem right, or true to the voice of the project. Which is why I found myself writing a new title for the same story at the top of the page in my notebook:

The Gospel of Us

What follows in this book is what I wrote next. The voice of a first-person narrator grown from and formed by Port Talbot; a fictional character I created and then let loose through the action of a play I'd written but not yet seen. NTW published the text in three pamphlets, each released on the morning of that day's performance. As a writer this proved to be a unique experience. To sit in a pub and watch nine or ten people reading and talking about a fictional scene in which they themselves had just played a part. This was, though, typical of the nature of *The Passion*, and was always at the heart of what we'd hoped to create, even as far back as when Michael, Lucy and I first met in that room two years earlier. A maelstrom of an experience in which the audience would be both witness and participant; three days of performance where ideas of place, history, fiction, theatre, life would all intersect within a single town before coming to a climax on a darkening roundabout beside the sea.

Book One: Friday

I realise I'm not someone you'd normally listen to; that usually you'd rather cross the street than risk hearing what I had to say – but you need to hear this.

Imagine me. My eyes hidden in the shadow of a hoodie, trackie bottoms, daps. The kid you recognise but never know; the kid with a dog slouch of a walk, a marble hardness in his eye. The kid who's half kid, half man. Who's stuck.

Don't expect me to be speaking like this, do you? Well, I never used to. But he changed all that. And that's why you need to hear this. Because this happened, and it happened here, to us. Believe me.

Whenever my bampa was down the social telling a

story, he'd pause before the best bits, lick his finger, touch it to his throat and then – so's you could only just hear him – whisper, 'God'shonesttruth now'. Then he'd carry on, making all those other men lean in over their pints and cans, listening.

Well, I'm licking my own finger now. And touching my throat. But it isn't God's Honest Truth what I'm going to tell you. It's ours.

If it begins anywhere, then it's with the man we came to call the Stranger. Still no one really knows who he was, or where he came from. But he came from somewhere and when he did, he came here, to the far end of the beach where the wind skates in across the bay to drive the dune grass crazy. That's where I first saw him. I used to go down that part of the beach on and off. End of the day, or start of it, letting that wind and the sea-light bring me round from whatever high I'd ridden or drink I'd sunk myself in the night before. He never talked to me, didn't even look at me. Just sat in this shelter he'd built, like a regular Crusoe, playing his guitar and singing to himself. At first I stayed well back, sitting on one of the dunes behind him, or on the wall in front of the Naval. But after I'd seen him a few times, I began to move closer, and that's when I heard what he was saying. And I wasn't the only one either. Every time I went down there, there were more of us, all moving slowly closer to him each time. No one speaking. Everyone just listening. Not that he was speaking or singing to us. No. It was the sea he was talking to, or just above it anyway, where the sky looks like water, or the water like sky.

When the slate falls,
when the crowned head drops,
when the sail is hoisted,
the earth shall give them up.
From the fire beneath the cross
the treasure shall be released
and the dead shall live
and the living shall be heard
and the heard shall be freed
and the freer shall be dead.
What was hidden shall be shown.

What was silenced shall be said.
What was forgotten shall be known.

That's how it went for a week. More people each day at dawn and dusk, under sun, rain and moon, and the Stranger singing his song to the sea. That's how it went. Until the morning of the Arrival, when everything changed.

The town was getting ready to welcome the Company Man. ICU was sending him here to make an announcement, and the Council and the Mayor had been getting themselves in a right twist about it for months. They wanted to show him a proper welcome, show him they had things handled down here, under control. That there was no need to go back to the bad old days when things had all got so bloody heavy-handed.

The preparations had been building for a week by then – platforms, welcome banners, bands practising flourishes and anthems. As the sun came up and I took my regular place in the dunes at the Stranger's camp, I could still hear the carpenters' hammers echoing up the beach. I'd been up all night, dropped a few tabs and I wanted to take some time out, hear him sing again, before I went home and tried to sleep. But as I sat down I saw something was different. The Stranger's song had changed, and he wasn't singing to the sea anymore but towards the Swansea end of the beach, towards the dunes and the grasses there.

He is come,
the empty vessel that will fill,
the one voice made of many
the man-key who will turn
the one who will release them
and heal us with his hearing
who will make us remember
what we'll never forget.
He is come.

All of us there, the crowd around his camp, we all looked to where the Stranger looked. Looked at the empty beach, his voice and the fizz of the waves filling our ears. There were more of us than usual; new faces had joined the regulars. Some had come because they'd been told about the Stranger; others were just passing. An early surfer, his wetsuit half peeled and his board under his arm; a woman walking her dog; a jogger, damp sand sprayed up the backs of his legs. All of us, motionless, looking down the empty beach.

Then, suddenly, the beach wasn't empty any more. There was a man. A man standing on a dune looking back at us; beard to his throat, wild hair stuck with bracken, clothes ragged and smeared.

When the Stranger saw him he stood up. The man was staring at him, couldn't take his eyes off him, like he was trying to remember where he'd seen him before. The Stranger though, he was as cool as you like, like this was all arranged. Like this was what he'd been waiting for.

For a minute or so they just carried on looking at each other. Then, moving awkwardly, like a man much older than he was, the Newcomer began walking down the dunes. When he got to him, the Stranger took him by the hand and led him down to the water's edge. Once there, the Stranger began undressing him, just started unpeeling the Newcomer right there and then on the beach. His skin was as white as a strip light. Dirty hands like gloves, a dove's collar of grime round his neck. Then the Stranger undressed too, leaving his clothes in a pile on the sand. And then they walked in, walked right on into the sea.

So, there they are, these two men, staring into each other's eyes, the foam of the waves washing round their waists, and all of us watching them. Eventually the Stranger breaks his stare and starts washing the Newcomer, scooping up handfuls of seawater over his arms and shoulders. All of us, meanwhile, begin walking down towards them. Which is when I see the two women and the little girl.

They were still far down the beach when I saw them, not as far as the preparations for the Company Man, but far enough so it was just their white nightdresses that shone out. I couldn't see their faces, but

I could tell their ages from the way they moved. An old woman on the left, a little girl, no more than nine or ten in the middle, then a younger woman on the right. They were walking towards us, holding hands. And they weren't the only ones either, because coming off the road was a chain of old men and women, shuffling down the road and up onto the beach. From the Home they were, Ysbryd Y Mor, in dressing gowns, slippers, nightdresses and pyjamas. Some of them couldn't have set foot outside for years, but there they were in the dawn light, the three cranes of the harbour standing to attention behind them, the whole town stirring from under the shadow of the mountain and these old folks, up and about and coming down to the sea to join in the fun.

By the time they reached us the crowd had formed a big semi-circle at the water's edge, everyone watching the Stranger and the Newcomer. The old folks joined us, then so did the two women and the little girl, coming right into the middle of the semi-circle, silent as you like, to stand and watch what would happened next. Which was this.

Slowly, the Stranger took the back of the Newcomer's head in the palm of his hand, like a mother might a baby's. With his other he embraced him, supporting him at his back like a movie star preparing to dip his lady for a kiss. Sundogs lit up the sea in patches behind them; the wind blew spray up into the early air and the gulls circled above, calling. For a second, everything was still, the two of them never taking their eyes off each other's face. Then, suddenly, it wasn't. Using all his strength, as if he wanted to get rid of him forever, the Stranger pushed the Newcomer, eyes still open, under the water.

He was under for a moment, and for a life.

When he surfaced again the breath he took was like his first and when he lifted his head and looked at us, it was like he'd never seen people before.

The Stranger led him back onto the beach after that, where he dressed him not in the crazy mix of clothes he'd arrived in, but clothes given to him from the crowd. The surfer handed him his jeans; a young lad his blue hoodie; the woman with her dog,

her socks. And the Stranger dressed him in them.
Dressed him as tenderly as a lover, or a son dressing
his father.

Then the dance began. I don't know who started
it, where the first hip swayed or the first foot tapped,
but out of nowhere, people were dancing. The old
folks from the home, men, women, the surfer, the
jogger, all of them started dancing around the
Stranger and the Newcomer, dancing in a closing
circle that swept them up and took them on down
the beach. Everyone, dancing at dawn. Everyone, that
is, except the two women and the little girl. They
didn't dance. They just looked, standing in a line
in their white nightdresses, hands held, watching.
And I didn't dance either. My head was spinning, my
body was light and my heart was pounding. I didn't
understand anything and yet it had all made sense,
as if it was all meant to happen. Like the coming of
the tide or the setting of the sun. It was natural.
But it was also too much for me, so I hung back
while the old folks and the Stranger and the Newcomer danced their way on down the beach, and

the two women and the little girl watched, and the town beyond started to wake, unaware of the storm approaching it.

The next time I saw the Stranger and the Newcomer it wasn't in person, but on paper. Along with most of the town I'd gone to the welcoming preparations for the Company Man down at the other end of the beach. There isn't much love for ICU here, nearly every lad with a pocket full of plectrums has written some kind of a song having a go at them. But they were in charge back then so there was a three-line whip from the Council to turn up. And to be honest, sod all else normally happens, so of course we were all going to have a look-see, weren't we? Besides, the closest people like the Company Man usually ever get to us is when they drive over the Passover, when a few wisps of smoke from our fires might brush against their tyres or whiff in through the fans on their dashboards. So, yes, if he'd come to talk, then we were going to listen.

Anyway, so there I was, milling around the crowd, looking for a loose pocket to pick, when I saw the

Stranger and the Newcomer again. At first I didn't know it was them. There was just this worried-looking woman, all frowns and concern, bloodshot eyes from crying, suddenly there in front of me shoving a piece of paper into my hand. 'Have you seen him? My son?' she was saying. 'Have you seen him?' Not that she stayed for an answer. Didn't pause even – went straight on to the next person, pushing another piece of paper on them, and then the next, and the next. There were two lads with her, trailing behind and looking equally concerned, but more for her than for the son she was asking about.

I looked down at the paper. MISSING, it said in big letters at the top, FOR FORTY DAYS AND FORTY NIGHTS. Then there was a photo, blurred and grainy, from CCTV from the looks of it – two men walking through the shopping centre, deep in conversation. One of them with his head circled and brighter than the other. Underneath the photograph it said:

Last seen with this man in Aberafan Shopping Centre. Local teacher, missing for over a month. If you have any information please contact his family on 07927 935215.

I looked at the photograph again. And that's when I saw it was them. The Stranger and the Newcomer. The Stranger didn't look too different. Had the same beard and everything. But the Newcomer, this teacher, well, he looked like a stranger to himself. Clean shaven, hair slicked back, smart jacket and shoes. But it was him; I was sure of it. Something in the eyes, in the way he was looking at the Stranger. It was him.

I looked up for the woman and her two sons. But the beach was packed now, and getting busier every second. So I turned back towards the town and, elbowing and shoving and squeezing between bags and bodies, made my way up to the steps by the slipway. Get some height I thought, see if I can't see her down there, making her own way through the crowd.

The beach was a crazy sight from up there. Thousands of people spread over the sand, right down to the water. Lines of local police in front of the slipway, welcome banners snapping and humming in the breeze, bands practising on the steps, the Mayor and the Councillors being shown where to stand so they could best lick the Company Man's arse. And that was just the obvious stuff. When I looked harder other, more secret stories made themselves known.

The teacher's mother wasn't the only person handing out pieces of paper. The local Resistance boys were at it too. Not as publicly of course, but they were there, weaving through the crowd, slipping flyers into pockets, pulling people to one side for a whisper in the ear or to press a folded pamphlet into a palm. Wasn't like they were going to miss a chance like this. They probably knew what the Company Man was coming to speak about already, and somehow I doubt what was on those flyers was a letter of support.

Further off I saw Simon my old music teacher from school, coaching some of the choirs. Old Alfie was there too, making a rare appearance from his house on Llewellyn Street. And Maggie as well, trying it on with the men, bold as brass, right in front of their wives sometimes, sniffing after any opportunity she might get to earn a few quid round the back of one of them stalls. Seemed like the whole town was out that day, buzzed up with anticipation. But no sign of the teacher's mother any more. And no sign of him, either.

Yet.

I was still standing on the steps by the slipway when I saw Uncle Bryn doing the rounds with his wooden staff and his puppet show. Now I remember Uncle Bryn from way back. Regular entertainer he was, bringing his shows to kids parties, dos at the social or sometimes, like today, down on the beach. I hadn't seen him for ages, but I suppose the Company Man's arrival had offered the chance for all sorts to put themselves in front of a crowd again and see if they still had it in them.

He was doing his show like he always did, building the whole thing right there – the stage, the little curtain, the piece of velvet he'd kneel behind. A good crowd had gathered round him, and not just kids either. But like I said, Uncle Bryn goes way back, so I'm sure there was more than one parent who'd come for their own memories more than their children's.

At the same time Uncle Bryn was doing his show another one was underway at the bottom of the slipway. A 'Pageant of Port Talbot' it was called, something the Council dreamt up by way of entertainment to keep everyone occupied while we waited for the Company Man. It was shit. Bunch of am-dram types cranking through a series of tableaux about the history of the town. Or rather *a* history of the town, because I don't remember seeing any scenes about the Passover being built above the rubble of my nan's house, or the coughing we used to get after playing footie under the towers of the chemical works, or the brown bags of cash that signed this shore away for industry not the resort it could have been. No, this was the official history. All polished up and lovely. At least it was until something happened to it.

The Mayor had stepped up to the microphone

again, making another announcement about how he was sure the Company Man would be 'here any minute, yes any minute now'. He looked terrible, all pale and shaky. Casting his eye over the scene he'd spotted Uncle Bryn below him, right smack in the path of where his honoured visitor was going to walk up from the sea. Still on the microphone he called down to him...

'Excuse me. You can't be there. Can you move out of the way please? We have a very important visitor coming. You're going to have to move. Who are you anyway? Is he one of yours, Simon? Do we know you?'

The Mayor waved over at Sergeant Phillips.

'Sergeant Phillips, can you...?'

But he got no further. Uncle Bryn had turned round when the Mayor'd called to him then, slowly, he'd lifted his staff to point it at his face. As soon as he did the Mayor froze. Stock bloody still, mouth half open. Sergeant Phillips was still bearing down but as Uncle Bryn started a slow turn, his staff outstretched, he was for it next. Then the next person, and the next. Soon Uncle Bryn had the whole crowd frozen, including me. The whole crowd, that is, except for those am-dram pageant actors who he didn't so much as have frozen, as had them completely. Like his puppets they were.

I know that sounds weird, *frozen*, but it's the only way I can describe it; as if the whole town was asleep but awake, sharing a dream. A dream that became a nightmare as the pageant actors, conducted by Uncle Bryn, played out a vision of pain and fire and voices and ghosts and hammers and doors and nails and gunshots and cheering and weeping and a death and a light and an ending that became a beginning.

You had to be there to understand what I'm saying, and I didn't even understand any of it then. All I do know is that it all started with Uncle Bryn. If I was my bampa, then this is when I'd be licking my finger and touching my throat again. It was him who was pulling the strings on this vision see – old Uncle Bryn, pulling the strings on all of us. Except it wasn't. Because just before I froze, I caught a glimpse of him, full on. And you know what? The man with the puppet show and the staff, he wasn't Uncle Bryn at all. It was the Stranger, that's who it was, dressed up as Uncle Bryn, grinning away, playing us all.

It was the flare that brought us round. Fired from one of the Company Man's RIBs, high and arcing up over the sea, bursting into purple. That was the sign he was on his way and all the Mayor and the Council needed to get them even more worked up than before. As soon as it burst everyone started moving again. I looked around, wanting to know if anyone else had seen what I'd just seen. But they all looked normal, or almost normal, as if maybe a flash of something had grazed their retina, but nothing else. And now I come to think of it, although at the time I knew I'd seen that vision, I also didn't know I'd seen it. Only later, much later, did I really remember.

The soft thud of a helicopter began to rise over the sea. The Mayor looked out to the water and saw the first of the RIBs cutting over the swell towards us, their snub noses in the air, their edges frilled with security. Clearing his throat he spoke into the microphones again, his voice watery at the edges.

'Here he comes! Here he comes! Now, I don't need to tell you again what an important day this is. So please, let's welcome our guest with open arms and open hearts and open minds, shall we? After all, as the Company's slogan says, ICU are "Looking Out For Your Future!"'

The police tried to get the crowd to meet his last words with a cheer, but the helicopter was in sight by now, so everyone was more interested in that, and the ten RIBs speeding over the water towards the beach. The first ones hit the sand like bullets, skidding up onto the shore, ICU security details jumping out, running through the crowd, planting flags to mark out a path. Others fanned out to secure the peri-meter, guns cradled against their bodies. Then came his bodyguards, black suited, speaking into their cuffs, scanning the crowds from behind dark glasses.

I looked towards the edges of the crowd again, saw the Resistance boys putting their hoods up, melting into the people milling around the stalls. As one of them backed away he put his hands to his mouth.

'Don't listen to them!' he shouted. 'They aren't interested in this town, only in what's under it!'

He must have thought he was far enough off to get away with it, but he wasn't. The crowd around him moved faster than fish from a shark, leaving him suddenly alone in a hole. Before he knew it two of Sergeant Phillips' police were on him, yanking his arms up his back, cuffing his wrists, putting gloved hands over his mouth. And as ever, in seconds he was gone. Dragged away to where the Company couldn't see him, his trouble or the punishment he'd get for it.

Back on the slip the bands had started up, and a choir too, singing for all they were worth as the Company Man, flanked by his suits, PAs and security, made his way up towards the Mayor. A right slick one he was. As neat and put together as a file folder, grin like a slash of steel, body tightly packed and well held. Eyes like lasers. Didn't miss a trick that one. No wonder the Mayor was bricking himself.

As the Company Man reached the slipway the band and choir reached their crescendo, then fell silent. He shook some of their hands as he passed, nodding and thanking them then, giving a neat little nod to the Mayor and Council too, he stepped up to the microphones. And then he waited. Oh he knew how to draw us in alright, just like my bampa down the social. Only there was no licking of fingers or touching of throats with this one, just him, staring out at us, over the town, over everything he controlled.

Now, I don't know if anyone else saw this, but as he stood there, I could have sworn I saw a flicker in his eye, like just for a second he'd caught something that wasn't meant to be there, something he perhaps didn't, after all, control. I followed his gaze up the sands, over the heads of the waiting crowd. And there they were. The two women and the little girl from the dance that morning, standing in a line far up the beach, their white nightdresses catching the sun, staring right back at him.

Never one to let himself be shaken, the Company

Man was soon back in charge, clearing his throat, leaning in slightly and speaking in that soft but firm father's voice of his. Lifting a hand, he acknowledged the smattering of applause.

'Thank you, thank you. It's such a pleasure to be here with you again, to be here in our town again, which, although it's been quite some time since my last visit, I can assure you, is never far from my thoughts. We have much to celebrate today. Five years of working together. Five years of a unique relationship, one of its kind in the entire world, between your town and ICU. Five years of building upon the skills of our separate pasts, so we may look towards our shared future.'

And that was as far as he got.

A woman's scream, then another. Shouts. A moving knot in the crowd, bodies pressing away from something. A man's loud voice, booming out of the PA system.

'Nobody move! Stay back! Back! This isn't a hoax, I'm warning you! This is real. Everyone stay still!'

ICU security, rifles at their shoulders, red sighting lasers skimming over the heads of the crowd. Then, like a pip spit out by the multitude, a woman, staggering onto the slipway, her body weighed down with packs and packs of explosives strapped about her chest.

Immediately those red lasers came swooping down. Like a starling shoal into a tree they nested in a cluster over her heart.

The man's voice again, 'Don't try anything! Shoot her and I'll detonate them. I will! I'm warning you! Stay back!'

The ICU security chief steps forward, Old Growler we used to call him, one hand raised high, stalling his shooters.

'Nobody move!' the voice shouts again.

And nobody does. For the second time in minutes we're all frozen, though this time we all know why.

The voice speaks again, a little quieter, but still hard and sharp as flint.

'A little closer, Joanne. And some more. That's it.'

He's talking to the woman. This woman who's

breathing like she's just run a marathon, her eyes swollen with tears. Following his orders she takes a few more faltering steps towards the Company Man. Close enough for the microphones to pick up the sound of her fear, short breaths, quick like a dying animal.

'Look at her. You, Company Man. Look at her.' The voice isn't shouting now. Just talking, right as if the person it belonged to was standing in front of him.

'She's a person. With a name, a life, hopes, memories. A person. Not just a figure in your spreadsheets. Not just a gradient on one of your graphs. She's an innocent person, like all of us. Like my mother was. Like this town. An innocent person in the hands of someone else, someone with their thumb on the detonator. So look at her, all of you, look at her. What I'm doing is no more than what *they* do every day. Because you've got us by the throats haven't you? You Company men have got your teeth deep in our throats, bleeding us working men dry. Until the day you choose to let go. And then what happens? We'll still die from the wounds you've left in us, just quicker, that's all.'

I look at the face of the Company Man. Not a flicker. His eyes are on the woman. I can tell he's thinking hard but I wasn't expecting him to do what he did next, to lean into the microphones and try to speak back to the voice.

'You don't have to do this,' he said, using his calm, older-brother tone. 'We can talk. Let her...'

'Shut it! Don't you dare tell me what I have to do!' The voice was back to shouting. As if that's what he'd been waiting for all his life, the chance to close this man down, to tell him what he thought of him, straight to his face.

'What do you know? What do you really know? Of course I have to do this. What else have we got left? Nothing else will make you listen! Nothing else will make *them* listen! Someone's got to make the sacrifice! Because this is all you understand isn't it? Domination, control, manipulation. ICU? Oh, I see you alright. You and that false council around you. I see you and your stories, your lies.'

The police must have spotted him and were trying to edge in, because the voice changed again. From shouting to threat...

'I told you, try anything and I'll do it. I will, I'm warning you I will!'

Other voices now, also shouting from behind. I turned round and saw where he was, up on the balcony of the Surf Lifesaver's Club. A man all in black, face covered, one arm held high, a pack of police, crouched down, guns raised, shuffling nearer to him.

Then all hell breaks loose and suddenly everyone's shouting. Old Growler barking orders into his radio, the bomber on the balcony, the police around him. Down on the slip, meanwhile, Joanne's breaths are become screams. Short, tight screams becoming the words of a woman expecting to die as the crowd around her keeps edging away, expanding a growing circle of alone, just her and the Company Man left at its centre.

BALCONY: I told you! Stay back! Stay back!

SLIPWAY: Oh please. Help me... help me. Please...

POLICE: Put it down! Put the detonator down!

GROWLER: Have you got a clear shot? Have you?

BALCONY: Don't come any closer! I'll do it! I will! I'm going to do it! I'm warning you! I am! I am! I am...

And then, from somewhere much further away, another voice. Level, calm, a note of relief.

'I see you.'

I think he came from the sea, from behind the crowd, but I still can't be sure. All I know is that suddenly he was there. The Teacher from those MISSING flyers. There on the slipway walking into that empty space towards the Company Man and Joanne.

The whole crowd pressed further away as the red sighting lasers danced over his body.

'You!' the bomber's voice shouted. 'Stop there.

Don't come any closer!'

But he did. It was like he couldn't hear him, like he couldn't hear any of it, everyone screaming at him to stay back, to stop. He just kept on walking towards Joanne, talking to her. And she was talking back to him too, her face changing shape as she did, from fear, to confusion, to sadness and then, and I'm not kidding now, honest, to happiness. By that point he was right up with her, reaching out his hands towards that jacket of explosives, everyone at full pitch telling him to stop.

I didn't see what happened next. Like everyone else I turned away, ducked down, pressed myself against the sand. I was sure they were going to blow. But when I opened my eyes we were all still there, and when I stood up I saw it was over. The Company Man was being whisked away by Old Growler's men, the bomber was being dragged off the balcony by the police and Joanne, without her jacket of explosives, was standing on the slipway embracing the Teacher.

I heard the bomber one last time, as the police

pressed his head down into a squad car. He was shouting again, but at the Teacher this time, not the Company Man.

'You don't know what you've done!' he screamed, pushing a gloved hand from his mouth. 'You're part of this now! You're part of this!'

And then he was gone, bundled into the car by a fist of police.

Back on the slipway Sergeant Phillips had collared the Teacher and was questioning him. I moved nearer, wanting to hear those answers myself.

SERGEANT PHILLIPS: Name?

TEACHER: I... I don't know.

SERGEANT PHILLIPS: Where do you live? Address?

TEACHER: I don't know. I don't know where I live.

SERGEANT PHILLIPS: What do you mean? You homeless?

TEACHER: I don't know. The last thing I remember was coming onto this beach. Today. That's all.

SERGEANT PHILLIPS: Hold on. You're him aren't you? The teacher. The one who's been missing.

TEACHER: Am I? I don't know. I don't remember anything.

I wanted to step up then, tell them both what I'd seen that morning, about the Stranger, the ducking in the sea, the dance. But it was too late. ICU security were clearing the beach, checking IDs. I felt a shove in my chest, turned to see a gas-masked face.

'Move on kid, scram!' it said.

So I did.

When I looked back the beach was already half emptied. The Teacher was gone too, and Joanne. But his mother was back, along with her two sons. She was standing where he'd just been questioned by Sergeant Phillips, looking around her, wild in the eye. One of her sons was trying to pull her away. The other just looked on, looking sadder than anyone I'd ever seen. I was quite far down the prom now, up by the café, but the wind was blowing her words my way, so I could still hear what she said as she searched around her like a woman looking for something she'd dropped.

'He was here,' she was saying. 'Just now. I saw him. My son. He was here.'

It was evening before the Company Man was ready to address us again. The Mayor had told us where to assemble – in the town centre in the secure area. He'd come to the microphone down on the beach when the echo of the police sirens was still in the air, more sweaty and pale than ever. We'd need our ID cards, he'd told us. There would be checks, barriers, but still, weren't we the lucky ones the Company Man had agreed to stay?

So like I said, it was evening by the time we gathered to hear his announcement, the light drawing in, the hill behind the town growing black against the sky. They'd set up a big screen so we could all get nice and close to the Company Man's steel-slash of a smile. I managed to get in as far as the first barrier, but then no further. Only those with the right credentials were allowed in the next section. The Company's lackeys, family members of the Council, no one who was going to cause any trouble. ICU obviously weren't up for taking any more chances. And neither was Old Growler and his security details, the way they shoved us around, patted us down, took anyone who looked suspicious elsewhere.

But still we kept on coming. We wanted to hear the news, didn't we? It was meant to be about our future after all, that's what the Mayor had said. And that wasn't a word often used about our town back then. It might have been in ICU's slogan, but that was about the only time we ever saw it. We'd used to talk about our past once but even that seemed to have gone now; squeezed out by the roads, the works and the concrete. And how can you talk about a future without a past? Cleverest thing the Company ever did, that's what my bampa used to say – 'The cleverest thing. Made us forget where we came from, so as to make us blind to where we're going.'

Around seven o'clock they cranked up the lights on the stage so we knew something was going to happen. Then we heard the mics being tested – 'One, Two, One, Two.' And then, out of nowhere, mid-sentence, we heard something else – something we weren't meant to hear.

The voice was unmistakable. That soft-firm father's tone, knowing and unmoving, so certain of itself. Only this time he wasn't up on a platform talking to us. He was still backstage and talking to the Mayor.

'...how it is, I wish it could be different but the decision has been made. We've invested too much to back off now.'

'This isn't what we agreed.'

'The Company agreed nothing. Listen. We've said all along we're committed to bringing the best out of this town, and one way or another that's what we're going to do.'

'But you said it would only be the people in the path of the new Passover. Nowhere else.'

'I'm trying to make this easier for you, Griffiths. The sooner we can get people moving, the better. People are adaptable. Holding on to this place is just going to make it harder for them in the long run. If the Passover story helps get things going – wonderful. If not then my security forces will be more than happy to move things along.'

'Why can't you tell them the truth?'

'Because it won't help them to know the truth. Look, do you think a man wants to be told he's worth more dead than alive? Well this town is worth more empty than with people in it. That's the truth. Do you want to go out there and tell them that? We know there are huge untapped resources beneath this town. *That's* the truth.'

'All I am saying is...'

'Hold on, is this on? Is this...?'

Then the mics went dead. The crowd, though, had both heard enough and wanted to hear more. I felt them shoving from the back, wanting to get closer. Anti-ICU chants started up, 'ICU – Out For Your Blood!', sending police officers scuttling from the front barriers back towards the rear. I heard the thwack of truncheons against bodies, shouts, cries.

Eventually it died down, the whole crowd settling like one restless animal. More lights came up on the stage and finally the Mayor appeared, looking even more shaken than usual. When he spoke to us, it was like he was only halfway there.

'The Company Man will now make his... announcement. Please listen very carefully to what he has to say. Thank you, and...'

He trailed off and just stood there, looking out at us all. Then he walked away. Nothing more, just walked away, shaking his head.

When the Company Man appeared, some of the chanting began again but it soon ebbed away. There was something in the way he looked over a crowd that made you want to quieten down, to listen. Like what he said would mean something for everyone – not necessarily in the words he used, but in how the shadows of those words might fall.

'Thank you. Thank you,' he said, though no one

was cheering. 'I am glad to see so many of you here this evening – so many of you undeterred by the unfortunate events of this afternoon. Let us be clear. What we were all witness to was an act of pure cowardice. An act of terrorism. Perpetrated, the criminals will *say*, in your name. But why? Why did these people try to silence us? I will tell you. Because these people, who say they are acting in your name, are afraid. That is why. And what are they afraid of? What can be so terrible that they will murder, maim and kill? They are afraid, my friends, of the very word I was using when we were so rudely interrupted. They are afraid of the future. But I know this town better than that. I know what you are made of, and I know that where they are cowardly you are brave. Where they are cruel you are kind and where they have fear, you have hope!'

From somewhere a few cheers. They might have been at the prod of the security's guns, but maybe not. Because you had to give it to the Company Man, he could speak. Oh yes, he could speak alright. He looked over us again, waited for the cheers to fade, then continued.

'Every age has had its enemies of progress. And in every age, these people have eventually been defeated. So I am here today to assure you that in our age, in our time, in our town, the enemies of progress, the enemies of the future, the enemies of enterprise *shall* be defeated. What, you may ask, makes me so confident? Because I know this town. This is a town ready for change. This is a town ready to embrace the bold new vision I bring before you today.

'And this is what I really came to speak to you about. Hope. Hope for a better future for all of us. We all know though, that however high we might hoist its sail, Hope will only ever take us so far without the winds of hard work and sacrifice to drive it.

'So this is also what I came to talk to you about today. Sacrifice. You and the generations before you have worked hard for this town. You have delved into the belly of the earth to bring forth steel, you have carved into the mountain's side to bring forth coal and *you* have harvested the sea at your doorstep to bring forth fish. Now after all those years of hard work, what I am proposing is that we allow the town to work hard for you instead. How? With the brave new vision of the future we call "The Passover Project". It is with great pleasure that I can reveal to you today that what we began with the construction of the M4 Passover road, ICU will bring to perfection with a new Passover Project. A great new road leading this town into a glorious future. A road that will increase the speed of transport links in this area by over sixty per cent.

'This road, like the first Passover, will be built over this town. It will bring work, it will bring jobs and it will bring investment. The promise of this Passover is our hope. So what then is our sacrifice? Only the same sacrifice this town has already borne so nobly in the past. Those living in the path of the Passover will have the opportunity to leave their old homes and move into new dwellings, purpose-built by the Company. This will not affect many of you. It will be a sacrifice borne by only a few, and we must applaud those brave and selfless enough who have already begun, with an eye to this town's future, to leave their old homes for pastures new. Some will be returning to their relatives in the countryside. Others will be housed by us, the Company. But all, I assure you, will be catered for.'

The timing was perfect. No sooner had the Company Man said those words than the first families began arriving outside the perimeter fences. Wrapped in blankets, carrying bags and boxes of belongings. Men and women, children and grandparents, a shuffling chorus of tired and angry faces, their lives in their arms, their worlds in pieces at their feet. Some of them began shouting at the Company Man through the fence.

'You lying bastard!'

'They're taking the doors! They're taking off the doors!'

'They came with guns! Told us to leave!'

'They took our front door, just ripped it off!'

'They're doing the whole street, the whole street!'

It didn't take Old Growler long to have his men over there, the familiar swift tide of black riot gear followed by silence.

The Company Man, though, took it all in his stride. 'Please,' he said, his arms held out to pacify us. 'Don't be alarmed. Clearly there's a certain amount of confusion. Some initial difficulties are only to be expected. I'm sure you understand a project like this is a huge undertaking and the road may be a little bumpy at first. I'll leave it to your Mayor and Council to distribute the necessary information but I wanted to bring you the good news myself. And to assure you that with this new Passover Project, the Company and I will continue "Looking Out For Your Future".'

He should have known better than to end with that. Showed how much he really knew us, how he had no idea that line was like a red rag to a bull for the protesters at the back. 'Don't believe them!' they shouted in response. 'Tell us the truth! The truth, the truth, the truth!' Then the familiar chant began:

'ICU – Looking out for themselves!'

'ICU – Looking out for themselves!'

The Mayor stepped forward and tried to say

something but it was clear no one was going to listen to him, so the Company Man came back to the microphone. This time, though, he looked different. Not so much ruffled, as angry.

'I want to speak to our enemies now,' he said, his eyes bright in the arc lights, his finger stabbing out at us. 'The enemies of this town. I know you're out there. I see you. Well, hear me now! You're a cancer on this town. A plague. And I will not rest until you have been driven out of this place, never to return. If anyone here, anyone, has any suspicions about who these enemies may be, where they may be gathering, what they may be plotting, then come forward. I urge you, no matter who you suspect – it could be a neighbour, a friend, even a member of your own family – come forward. You can alert any one of my security forces – here to protect you – and they will be more than willing to assist.'

It was all the crowd needed. His words were like flames to blue touch paper. Together with what we'd heard from backstage, his slick speech, the news of the Passover Project, the families at the fence, this call to snitch was the final straw. The Resistance boys saw their chance and were soon sliding through the crowd like eels, stoking the fire, starting the chants, stirring it up. The police tried to keep control, but the crowd was too strong for them, so ICU security came in too, which only made it worse. Everyone was surging forward, forward, trying to get closer to where the Company Man stood up on the platform. I saw a woman start climbing the barrier fence in front of us. She was shouting as she climbed.

'What do you want? What's under this town? Tell us the truth!'

Her face was twisted in anger, in fear. She was shouting at the Company Man, boring her eyes into him, so she didn't see Old Growler down below her. Didn't see him take a pistol off one of his men and start striding towards her; didn't see him raise that pistol, both arms straight; didn't see his finger squeeze on the trigger.

I saw the shot before I heard it – a sudden wound of blood and broken bone erupting between her shoulder blades. And then the echo of it, resounding between the civic buildings, stopping the chants, the shouts dead.

She fell like a bird from a tree.

Slow at first, then a heavyweight descent, tipping backwards into the screams of the crowd. I turned away, expecting to hear the thud of her body hitting the ground. But it never came.

When I turned back the crowd had cleared from around her, everyone pressing back in a circle, edging away from her death. Everyone, that is, except for the man who'd caught her.

Straight away spotlights were on them, and a camera crew, catching her last breath in his arms as he looked down into her face, his own obscured under a blue hoodie. The front of her chest was crimson, as was the ground beneath her, blood pouring from her back. She was shivering, shaking, so the man, still holding her in his lap with one arm, took off his hoodie with the other and laid it over her.

For a moment nothing else happened. It was like they were painted there, lit in the lights, her head resting against his shoulder, her arms hanging limp, her knuckles resting on the ground. But then he lifted his head, and we all saw it was him.

The Teacher, clear as daylight, with that camera zooming in close now to shine up his image on the big screen behind us.

Staring through the barrier fence he looked towards the Company Man, still stood at his microphone on the platform. The Company Man returned his gaze. Eventually it was he who spoke first – not to the crowd, but just to the Teacher.

'Who are you?' he said. The Teacher looked confused, before trying to answer.

'I'm... I am...'

But he got no further.

The Company Man filled the silence again.

'If you have something to say, then say it.'

The Teacher looked blank. He looked down at the woman, dead in his arms, then up at the Company Man once more.

'I have nothing to say,' he said. 'I came to listen.'

Book Two: Saturday

Before I tell you what happened that Saturday, I should tell you what else happened on the Friday night first. I don't know why, but a few hours after that woman was shot, I went back to the secure area in the centre of town. It was dark by then, the big arc lights turned off, the civic buildings inking round the square like sleeping giants. ICU security and the police were still there, but unseen, in the shadows. The whole place was like a forgotten memory, as if whatever we did, whoever died, none of it would ever be noticed.

But not everyone had forgotten. I knew that as soon as I entered the square and saw the candles. I don't know who'd brought them, but there they were, a huddle of them all different sizes, their wax melting down their sides like tears. They'd been placed right where she'd fallen and right where he'd caught her. I walked closer to them. Their flames lit the ground so I could still see the stain of the woman's blood, spreading like the map of a country over the paving slabs, cities and towns marked in dark spots of old chewing gum. Like I said, I still don't know who'd put them there, who'd lit them, but it was enough that they did. Not forgotten, that's what those flames said. Still burning and not forgotten.

I knelt down to feel their warmth against my hands. It was a gentle heat, like a breath or human blood. As I crouched there I listened to the night-time town. It was death-bell quiet – just the usual sighs of cars and lorries over the Passover and somewhere else, streets away, a security alarm com-plaining. It was like the whole town wasn't so much sleeping quiet as waiting quiet. Waiting for the morning, for this night to be done and for it all to begin again.

I stood to go and that's when I saw the other light. Far away, up on the mountain. Just a lamp probably, hung on a tree, but strong. A low star speaking to those candles at my feet, like a beacon. I knew right away it was him. Up there for the night with his new followers. And I knew, too, that the lamp was only that – a lamp, to help them cook, wash, see. But as I walked away, because of everything else that had happened that day I knew it wasn't just a lamp either, was it? It was like those candles, that light up there – a memory, a not-forgotten, a sign that somewhere at least things were still burning.

I slept like a log that night. Slept like I'd never slept before, body sunk right through the mattress type of sleep. So first I knew about the new day was my phone kicking off somewhere under my clothes on the floor. Fumbling around, I found it and looked at its screen. It was my buttie Johnny over on Llewellyn street. I was late for band practice, that's what he said. 'Band Practice'. I had to laugh, we weren't no band, at least not yet, not then. Johnny'd bought some drum kit up the valleys the week before, fifty quid for a mint set, never been used, 'kept in towels the whole time butt,' Johnny said. Anyway, as far as he was concerned, that was enough. We'd be a band. Him, me and little Evs Bach. Fair dos, he'd had worse ideas, so I'd said I was up for it. He was still dead keen about the idea and I didn't want to let him down so I climbed out of bed, threw on my clothes and made my way over to Llewellyn Street.

At least, that's where I'd thought I was going. To the same old Llewellyn Street I'd always known – one row of pebbledash, flat-face terraces facing up to the pillars of the Passover. But I wasn't, was I? The way there might have been the same – same pavements, same streets, same alleyways and underpasses. But the destination, well, that both was and wasn't the same, like the whole place had been pushed through the looking glass.

I saw the cricket game first. They were playing it in the street, but slow, like their bones were made of lead. Young lads, a few girls and some older men too, bowling and batting right there on the tarmac. Then, as if that wasn't surprise enough, I saw the other side of the street, the side that, ever since the Passover was built, hasn't been a side for years. And that, well, that stopped me in my tracks alright. To be honest, I thought I was having a flashback from a bad tab, until I realised that other people could see it too. And what could they see? Well, like I said, the other side of the street, there again, as if the concrete, bulldozers, cranes and trucks of the Passover had never been here at all. All of it was there, but ghosted. No walls as such, or roofs or windows, but the outlines of the houses were still there, along with their families inside them, watching telly, washing up, playing on the floors of their living rooms.

Imagine if you'd taken an x-ray of a whole street, then coloured it in with bright washing on lines, people's faces, rugs, carpets and radios. Well, that's what it was like. A demolished street brought back to life, not with the bricks that had built it, but with the families who'd lived inside them, back home at last.

I was still staring at that ghosted side of the street when I heard Johnny running up behind me, all panting and blathering.

'It was Alfie, no lie now. It was him who done it. I swear it. You've gotta believe me butt.'

I put my hands out, trying to calm him. 'Alright, Johnny, alright. Easy now. Now, what you sayin' 'bout Alfie?'

'It was him. As made the other side of the street.'

I looked back at the slow cricket game, a woman laying a table for dinner beside one of the fat pillars of the Passover, an old bloke reading his paper beside a fireplace, a kid building an Airfix plane on his bed. Then I looked back at Johnny, my head still spinning.

'What you on about Johnny?' I said. 'How did Alfie do all this?'

'I don't know,' Johnny said, all bulging eyes and high brows. 'But I'm telling you mun, he did. I saw him. I was out giving that stray some milk see, when I sees Alfie step out of his front door. I know he's always been an odd one, but he was looking even odder today, staring over there at the pillars. And not just staring either, but speaking too. So I goes nearer, didn't I? An' he was saying numbers and names, over and over, the numbers of houses and the names of the people who'd lived in them I reckon.'

I put my hands out again, stopping him. 'What makes you think that?'

'Because,' Johnny said, pulling himself up like this was his big moment, 'when he said their names, they arrived, didn't they?'

'Arrived? From where?

'I don't know,' he said, stepping closer to me, and dropping his voice. 'But they did. All of 'em. Just appeared from behind the pillars. An' that's what I mean. Alfie, it was him who done it, him who built the street again, just by talking.'

I looked back at the street. It was all too much, and too much of a coincidence too. This had to be the Teacher. I knew it in my bones. The Company Man was going to take more of the town away so, to piss him off, the Teacher, with a little help from Alfie by the looks of it, was bringing other bits of it back. I didn't know how, and like I said when you first came to listen to me, I still don't. But I just knew it, deep down. This, the cricket game, the terrace of dreams, it was all him.

So for once I wasn't surprised when I saw him. Because of course he was there, wasn't he? Just as he was always in the middle of things yesterday. Only this time, there wasn't just him. There were his followers too.

From what I could tell they'd started tagging along with him right from the start. Everyone knows that when he left the slip on Friday Joanne had followed him along the beach, stepping her feet in the prints of his. And we know, too, how he picked up Peter not long after, bumping into him when he was on his way back from fishing off the rocks at the end of the prom. But all the others? People find it hard to believe now, just how many there were. Bloody hundreds of them – most, by the look of it, fresh (or not so) off the mountain where he'd slept that night. He was walking out from one of the houses, one of the real ones mind, not one of Alfie's, towards the front door of another. Walking steady and slow just like any normal bloke taking a morning stroll, only this one happened to have a wedding train of people in his wake. And so many of them.

Old and young, men and women, poor and poorer.

I stepped away from Johnny to get a closer look at the Teacher. He looked the same as when I saw him yesterday, but different too. On the beach and then again in the secure area, he'd looked like a lost child. But now he wasn't. He was walking with direction, and there was a light in his eye. Not of knowing, but of wanting to know. Like he was starving for stories, for voices. Which, it turned out, he was.

I couldn't get into the house he entered. There was no room, what with the followers, the families who lived there, and now the TV crews too, the ones who'd come for the Company Man but who reckoned they'd sniffed out a juicier story with the Teacher. I still know what happened inside that house though because it all came back to us like Chinese whispers, running through the crowd like a voltage. How the Teacher had sat down and taken a cup of tea with the old woman who owned the house. How she'd told him her stories and then how everyone else did too. A blind boy. A young girl who cares for her mam. A mute girl, tapping out her tale

for him on the arm of her wheelchair. How all he'd
done was sit and listen, nothing else, and how,
somehow, that listening had been enough. How it
did something. How people came out of that house
lighter, like a weight'd been taken off them. Like
they'd been healed.

I was still standing at the back of that crowd, listening to the commentary filter through it, when I
heard other voices, further off, towards town. I
stepped away to try to hear them better, but still
couldn't make sense of them. It sounded like more of
a droning than a conversation, like the ebb and flow
of a hive. So I took a few more steps away from the
people milling around the house, walking, as I did,
through the imaginary walls of Alfie's dream terrace,
past a woman making a bed, a granddad struggling
with his braces.

From what I could tell the voices were coming
from over by the graveyards. And not just voices
either, but lights too. Flickering lights like a slow
strobe, flashing up under the underpass. Taking one

more look at the crowd behind me, I decided to go and see what was going on. Maybe, I thought, the Teacher had done one of his disappearing acts and was already at work over there by the graves, conjuring up some more of his listening brand of healing.

But I was wrong. There wasn't any kind of healing happening over by those graveyards.

Just hurting.

Legion we called them. The Legion Twins. Couple of scrawny kids living in the underpass between the cemeteries of St Mary's. No one remembers why they got that name. You know how it is with nicknames. Something you did as a kid, or your dad did, or your cousin way back, and bang, you're stuck with it. Well, theirs was the Legion Twins and always had been as far as I knew. Every town has people like them I reckon. That bloke you see every day, wandering round the streets, mumbling. You know who I mean, don't you? Might stick out a skinny hand now and then, ask you for change. Ever talked to him? No, course you haven't. Why would you? Can't get a bloody word in edgeways with them types, can you? So busy talking to themselves. And that's how it was with the Twins. We all knew them but no one ever spoke to them, and they never spoke to us either, just to themselves or to each other.

Turns out though, as I discovered when I came round the corner towards the underpass, we'd been wrong about the Twins all along. All those years they weren't talking to themselves but to them, the Dead. And to us, I suppose. The us we'd already forgotten. Even talking *for* us in a way. And we'd never known. Until that day, when coming round the corner and seeing them in the underpass hurting like that, it had all made sense.

I say sense, but that's not really the right word for what I saw. I'm not going to even try and explain it, so let me just describe it for you instead.

All through that underpass, the same one I'd walked through a thousand times before, the Dead were coming out of the ground. Not in that Zombie way mind, not like in a film, but *in* film. Home movies, that's what those flickering lights were. Home movies coming out of the ground, hitting the walls and roof of the underpass, loads of them. Weddings, christenings, children's birthday parties, a boxing match, long-gone families and friends. Some in black and white, others in 60s and 70s colour. It was like a kaleidoscope under there, it was. A swirling kaleido-scope of gone lives in a gone town. Some of them were only coming partway through, squeezing their light through a tiny hole in the ground. Others, though, were on full show, shining from great big gaps in the tarmac, as if it was the pressure of the years that had pushed them through. But it hadn't. Not on its own anyway. It was the old Legion Twins that had let them through, you see. I'd never seen them move so fast. Running from here to there, panting, manic-eyed, one carrying a big old pickaxe, strong as a miner, the other just working with his hands – doing whatever they could to open up that tarmac and let more of those memories out from under it.

I stood there watching them, sweating and strained, panicked. It was like their lives depended on getting those films out from under there, as if this was their one chance and unless they set them free it was all over. As I watched they started talking again, the same old Legion Twins mumble and mutter.

Only this time, for once, I listened.

'Not forgotten, not forgotten,' said one of them.

'The last death is your name said for the last time. Name. Find the name,' said the other.

'So many under, so many under,' said both of them. 'Must get them out. Get them out.'

And that was when, as if in reply, those voices started up again.

It was like someone had turned up the volume on a hundred radios all at once; hundreds of voices, high, low, young, old, all speaking together and against each other. From where I was in the underpass I couldn't work out, at first, where they were coming from. But as they got louder that soon became clearer. The graveyards. The voices were coming from the graveyards around the church.

BOOK TWO: SATURDAY

As soon as they started one of the Twins clamped his hands to his ears, pressing them hard against his head.

'Arrgghhh,' he screamed. 'I can hear one, I can hear one!'

'Go, go!' his brother shouted back at him.

And he was off, sprinting into the graveyard, while his brother ran to the wall of the underpass, picked up a piece of chalk and stood there, poised, ready to write. I didn't know what was happening, but whatever it was, I didn't want to miss it, so I ran after the first one, into the graveyard.

It was the Dead again, only this time not in film, but in person.

There was one of them standing beside every gravestone, standing in crooked lines like chess pieces in a half-played game. They weren't moving, just standing there, speaking. At first I couldn't make out what they were saying, all their voices mixing together in that drone. But when I stepped nearer to them, I realised they were telling stories. Each one telling a story about whoever's name was carved on the stone beside them. Not stories of their deaths either, of how they'd died, but of their lives and how they'd lived.

I looked over to where the first Legion Twin was hurrying between them all, hands still at his head, pausing by each person, leaning in to listen – to a little girl, to an old man, to a young woman.

'Find them! Find them!' his brother called from the underpass.

He ran faster, searching between the stories, listening to the voices outside and inside his head. 'Loved... loved... loved John the most! John the most! Where are they? Where are they?'

Then he stopped. All of a sudden, he stopped beside a grave where a little boy was reciting the poem of his life, over and over.

'Dewi Phillips!' he cried. 'Dewi Phillips! Write it! Write it!'

I looked over to the underpass where the other Twin was searching now, searching for space on the underpass wall which was already scrawled with thousands of names.

'Can't find space! Can't find space!' he yelled back, panicking.

'Arrghhh,' his brother replied. 'Quick, find space! Find space!'

Then from the underpass, 'Writing! Writing!'

And as he did, the voices faded down, his brother took his hands from his head, and, standing up straight again, strolled over to his twin under the road.

'Ta,' he said. 'Ta very much.'

'No problem,' his brother replied, slipping the chalk in his pocket. 'Tidy.'

And that's when it dawned on me. It was like what Johnny had said about Alfie on Llewellyn Street. What I was seeing and hearing was what the Legion Twins had always seen and heard. All of it, the memories under the ground, the stories of the lives of the dead, all of this was what the poor sods had been carrying around with them for years until now, finally, it was out, out for all to see.

I had to go get Johnny. I wanted him to see this too, wanted to know *if* he could see it too. But I was too late. Coming out of the graveyard I ran straight back into them all – the whole crowd from Llewellyn Street, rushing into the underpass. They must have heard the voices too, I guess, and seen the lights of the films. Or at least the Teacher had, and let's face it, wherever he went by then, whatever he did, so did that crowd. I looked around for him and sure enough there he was again, already walking among those memories coming out of the ground, bathing in them, standing in their beams, allowing the gone faces and places to play all over him, to wash him in their flickering light.

I felt a tug on my sleeve and turned round to see Johnny.

'Have you seen this?' I said to him, throwing my arms at the underpass. 'And in the graveyards? The twins and everything? What's going on Johnny?'

'I don't know,' he said, waving his phone in front of me. 'But never mind this, we got to get over to the shopping centre.'

I looked at the screen of his phone. Someone had sent him a photo from the centre. At least, it looked

like it was from the centre but, just like Llewellyn
Street, it looked totally unlike the shopping centre
too. It was packed. Not just a busy Saturday either, I
mean totally roofed. I could make out huddles of
people in red blankets, makeshift stalls and stands, a
tower of old TVs and in the foreground a band playing on the roof of the café, all of them in balaclavas,
their faces hidden.

'When was this taken?' I asked Johnny. 'When's
this photo from?'

Pocketing his phone he leant in and, with that
sense of drama he'd come to love so much, whis-
pered into my ear.

'Now,' he said, low and hoarse, his voice all ex-
citement and wonder. 'That photo is now.'

We heard the shopping centre kicking off before we
saw it. It sounded like a mix of a music festival and a
prison riot, all amplified by the big echoing space of
it all, like the whole place had been turned into a
giant speaker.

There were that many people it was a job to get

inside. But when we did I knew right away this wasn't going to end well; that there was no way the Council, much less ICU would let what was happening in there go unnoticed or unpunished.

One part of the floor looked like a refugee camp. The Company Man obviously hadn't wasted any time with those plans of his, with his moving of people from their homes. But something must have gone wrong too. Because usually the Company wouldn't let us see the results of their dirty work, would prefer to brush them under the carpet or move them out of sight. But this time that hadn't happened, and that's why the camp on the floor of the centre was crammed with families and people who'd been chucked out of their homes. For once they hadn't gone elsewhere, but had stayed instead; not-forgotten, still burning. Some local groups had been handing out red blankets to them which just made them stick out even more, as if ICU had cut into the flesh, not the soil of this town, and these people flowing into this camp were its blood. Which, of course, they were.

All around that camp were the possessions they'd managed to bring with them. Not in piles, not just strewn about but ordered, arranged, like shrines. Their owners were quiet beside them, not kicking up a fuss or anything. As if they knew that by just being there, by not going away, by being in sight and therefore in mind, they were causing trouble enough.

The rest of the centre though, well, that wasn't quiet at all. Something – the assassination attempt on the beach the day before, the leaking of ICU's plans, the shooting of the woman, the Teacher – something had lit a spark that had lit a fire, the flames of which were now burning brightly in that shopping centre. Banners of protest, flash mobs of kids playing havoc with the Council police, banks of TVs showing testaments from the imprisoned and the disappeared. No wonder the Resistance boys were in there too. Must have thought it was their hour, their day, that finally the Town was going to listen to them and wasn't going to take ICU's messing lying down any more. The very fact The Band had turned up again, well, that was a sign of just how confident they suddenly were.

Still, no one really knows who The Band were, other than every now and then they'd crop up, sing their Resistance songs, then disappear again before the Council could get their hands on them. Always played in balaclavas, and hardly ever on a stage. Always somewhere they could cut and run if they had to – on a car-park roof, down some back alleyway, in the derelict cinema. I hadn't seen them for ages and, I'll be honest, I think we'd all assumed they'd been caught or disappeared. Or, like most everyone else, that they'd just given up. But they obviously hadn't, had they? And now they were back to prove it, back to help fan those flames which had caught all over town.

Like I said though, as soon as I'd seen the state of the shopping centre, all those people gathering, the protest stalls, the shrines of belongings, The Band, I'd known ICU wouldn't let it go on for too long before stepping in with their size nines. And sure enough, that's just what they did, a full raid on the place, about twenty or so pairs of size nines to be exact, all attached to the feet, legs and riot armour of ICU security, Old Growler at their head.

It was The Band they were after but as ever The Band were too quick. They'd set up their signaling chain before they'd started playing, and the call had come down the line a good few minutes before the security came barging through. So by the time they did The Band were already gone, just their kit abandoned on the café and the buzz of a single amp; that was all that was left of the song that had, just minutes before, been filling the place.

Seeing the security come in we'd all braced ourselves for what would happen next. But ICU must have been more nervous about what was happening than we thought, because there was no clearing of the place, no arrests, just regular ID checks, a few searches of bags and then they drifted away to the edges to keep an eye on everything from there.

The Company Man must have known he'd have to play this one subtly, I reckon – that he couldn't just come down hard again. That what was happening was something new, something different and as such he'd have to come up with something new and different himself to counter it. If only we'd known exactly how new and how different then we might have been able to stop it. Except of course, he never wanted it stopped, did he? The Teacher, I mean. Because he might have walked down that dune on Friday morning looking like a lost child, but by the time the shopping centre was kicking off, he already knew, I reckon. Somehow, from all he'd seen and heard, he already knew what was going to have to be done. And how he was going to do it.

Johnny and me hung around the centre for a few more hours after the raid, just to see what was going to happen next. But not much else did. It seemed like the happening had all slowed down for a bit by then, and in its place there was a sense of waiting instead; the whole town waiting for the next trigger, the next move – by us or by them, by the Company Man or by the Teacher.

We were on our way out, heading back to

BOOK TWO: SATURDAY

Johnny's to finally have that practice, when I got a clue as to what that next move might be. A flyer, palmed into my hand by a kid in a black hoodie, walking past me as quick as a whippet. By the time I looked round he was already gone, melted into the crowd.

'What's it say?' Johnny asked.

I looked down at the flyer. There was nothing fancy about it, no illustrations, printed in a hurry by the looks of it. Just some words on a page.

But that was enough.

TONIGHT

Sandfields Social and Labour Club

THE LAST SUPPER

Be There

They'd started closing the social clubs the year before all this happened. At first no one really noticed. After all, the kids and grandkids of the men who'd founded them had moved on to the pubs now, hadn't they? There were no Sunday drinking laws any more, so who needed them old clubs? The Naval, the Social and Labour, The Royal Legion. The first ones were taken under the story of property developers. The lights were turned off, the bar equipment sold off, the pool table auctioned off. Boards went up on the windows and the club went quiet, waiting for the bulldozers. Only the bulldozers never came. The 'development' never happened, as if those companies weren't developers at all, more like assassins.

It was around then, with people starting to complain, starting to miss the gone socials, that the Resistance realised the clubs left might still be of some use to them. Handy fronts for organising meetings, recruiting, getting their pamphlets out among the people. And it worked for a while too. Council didn't want to be going in and mess up a good honest working man's night, now did they? Not likely. ICU, however. Well, they weren't so touchy-feely about the clubs. They soon got wind of the connection between the socials and the Resistance. They had their people, their eyes, their ears, their spies. They had their cameras and their recording equipment, so no surprise when they started closing down the clubs themselves. No developer story needed any more either. Just straightforward 'support of an illegal organisation' notices, papers served, then sweetened a few weeks later with empty offers to set up meetings for a new 'leisure facility'.

By the time all this happened with the Teacher the Sandfields Social was the last club left in town. But even the Sandfields' time was up now. The committee had been issued with an eviction order and a hefty fine if they didn't comply. Like so much else they'd had to accept, but there was no way they were going quietly.

The party for the last night of the club had been planned ever since we got news of its closure. A proper send-off for the old girl, that's what the committee decided to do, and for the old boys who'd sailed in her for all those years, weaving their way across her floors, unsteady as regular sailors on a real ship at sea. And at first, that's all that night was going to be. The best bloody party the town had seen for ages; half celebration, half wake. But not any more. Not now, not with what was stirring in the town, with the shooting in the civic centre and with these crowds the Teacher was gathering. No, with all that going on the closing dinner had become something else instead. It had become the next move in this new game. And I'm telling you, after what I'd witnessed so far, there was no way in hell I was going to be missing it.

The club looked beautiful for her send-off. Fair dos, the committee had sunk their hearts and souls into this party, and, no doubt, the last of the club's coffers too. Now, nobody can say she's the prettiest looking thing from the outside, the Sandfields Social. I think even her most dedicated drinkers would have to admit that. Big lump of moulded plastic slumped at the end of a weed-ridden car park. But step through her swing doors upstairs and it turns out under that grey exterior she's only wearing the club equivalent of pink frilly knickers, isn't she? Decked out like a regular 70s crooners palace she is, little stage and all. And for the party that night they'd really gone to town. Fixed the lights, taped up the slipped gels, even got two big screens up and the old disco ball turning again, like a glittering moon above us all.

I was at the bar, staring up at that disco ball when I saw the balloons up there too. Helium balloons they were, in silvers and reds and electric blues, still stuck up against the ceiling from the parties gone by – an unofficial archive of all the moments marked in there. '60 Today!', 'Congratulations', 'Newly Weds', 'Happy 80th', 'Happy 21st', 'Happy 18th'. Yes, the Sandfields Social had been there for all of us at some point, giving all of us a little bit of escape and memories, if only for one night.

To begin with the closing party was just that, a regular party. A fair bit of crooning and even some old blokes getting up on stage to share their best memories of the place. There was food too of course, carried six plates to an arm by waiters out the banging swing doors of the kitchen, while the drink flowed from the taps so quick the barmen spent half their night down the cellars changing the barrels. Yes, a regular night in the social it was, with the volume and colour all turned up to make it the best night she'd ever seen.

But then the Teacher showed up. Whenever he did, trouble wasn't far behind, it hadn't taken us long to learn that one. So while he was welcomed with a cheer when he entered, a sense of unease shivered through the room at the same time too. He was with a bunch of his followers. At the time I didn't know this, but turns out they were the ones he'd approached to follow him, not some of the hundreds of randoms who'd done it the other way round. Being an old-time club man, Peter led them in, shouting across the room with the confidence of a lifetime membership.

'Garry? Garry! Just putting some of my mates up on the committee table. That alright? Great, champion, thanks Garry!' Then there was the Teacher himself, Joanne, looking all doey-eyed at him, Alfie from Llewellyn Street, the Legion Twins, Simon my old music teacher and, lastly, one of his brothers. The younger one, the sad-looking one from the slipway, only he didn't look sad any more.

I watched them from where I was propped up at the bar as they sat down round one long table. A regular dirty dozen they were, a right old patchwork of oddballs. As for the Teacher, well, I reckon I was one of only a handful who'd seen him from the very start, from that first moment when he'd appeared on the beach. As such I'd been able to track his changes from the beginning. And he was changing, make no mistake about it. Like he was living a full life in just a few days; learning and soaking up everything at the speed of light. It was in his eyes, that's where the change was happening. In the way he looked at us all, and the way he looked at his followers around him.

Or was it?

I still can't be absolutely sure, but in the years since it's crossed my mind more than once that perhaps he wasn't changing after all. That perhaps it wasn't him, but us. The way we looked at him, the way we saw

him, the way we watched him. Maybe, after everything, this whole story isn't about what he did to us,
but about what we did to him. Not for me to say,
I suppose. We all see things different, don't we?
Remember things different. You'll have to ask Johnny
for his version, or his mam, or anyone else who was
there. It's all different ways of seeing and believing
isn't it? And like I said, I still can't work out most of
it for myself – I'm just telling you what I saw and
felt, that's all, so don't shoot the messenger.

One thing's for sure though, the Teacher and his
followers were having a rare old time at that party,
no doubt about that. Tucking into the scampi, chips
and pints, laughing good and hard at Peter's stories
about how he'd vouched so and so into the club, and
him, and him. It sounds odd, I know, but for all their
strangeness they looked like a regular family up there.
A regular family enjoying a night out at the social. I
only mention this because the Teacher already had a
real family. For some reason though, apart from his
younger brother sat beside him now, he didn't want
anything to do with them. I saw as much just before

BOOK TWO: SATURDAY

I left the shopping centre with Johnny, just after that whippet boy palmed the Resistance flyer into my hand.

We were making our way into the street when I saw him again, the Teacher, down below among the red-blanket families and their shrines. No surprise there, I suppose, him sitting down with them, listening again. But what happened next, well that was a surprise alright.

I saw her coming through the crowd just before she got to him, moving as quick as she could, shoving people aside, wide-eyed, head moving from side to side to see around the bodies in the way. I recognised the desperate look on her right off, and the frowns of the two big fellas striding behind her too.

I grabbed Johnny by the arm to stop him. 'Hold up,' I said. 'She's found him.'

'Who's found who?' he said.

'The Teacher's mam,' I replied, pointing down at the shopping-centre floor just as she got to him. 'She's found him.'

When she did she flung her arms round his neck and buried her face in his chest as if she was drowning and he was the last piece of driftwood for miles.

'My son! Oh my son! I told them!' she cried into his shoulder. 'I said you'd come back. Where have you been? I knew it was you. My son!'

I'm telling you, the look on her when she pulled back – you'd have to be a hard-hearted bastard not to have welled up at it. She must have thought him dead and now all of a sudden, after all those months, here he was again, brought back to life, back with her at last.

One of the brothers, the older one, was soon pulling on her sleeve.

'Mam. Not here. Come on. Come on now.'

But she wasn't budging, not now she'd found him, so she clung on, weeping into his clothes. So the brother turned his attention to the Teacher instead.

'Look at the bloody state of her! Look what you done to her! Come on now, let's get out of here.'

BOOK TWO: SATURDAY

The Teacher glanced at him, but said nothing. Which is when his mam looked at him properly, really properly.

'There's something not right. Look at him. There's something not right.'

Then he said it. The worst thing she could have heard.

'Who are you? I... I don't know you.'

For a moment she was stunned, looking up into the face she'd watched all those years, only to see her own unrecognised in his eyes. When she finally spoke, it was through a scream, a primal, heart-wrung scream.

'Don't say that! Don't say that! I'm your mother! Your mother!'

Well, then it really kicked off. The older brother having a go at the Teacher, his mam pleading with him, and trying to stop her other son from shouting, everyone stopping and staring. To top it all the police had started clearing the centre, making announcements over the tannoy...

THE SHOPPING CENTRE WILL CLOSE IN THREE MINUTES. PLEASE VACATE THE BUILDING.

But you know what? In the middle of it all, in the very centre of that storm of people, the Teacher was still and calm as you like, with eyes for only one person; his other brother, the sad one from the slip.

I couldn't hear a thing by now, not from where we were up on the balcony, but I saw the Teacher speak to him, and the younger brother say something in reply, something that sent the older one even deeper into his rage, and made their mam grasp and grab at her hair.

It wasn't a pretty sight, so in a way I didn't mind that we had to start moving on. ICU security were locking the place down, so we had to head. But I wanted to know too. Why was he being like that? Why was he saying those things to his own mam? Shouting after her as the older brother dragged her away,

'Who are you woman? Who are you?'

And her replying, with all the anguish of a wounded animal,

'I'm your mother! I'm your mother!'

Again and again, her voice raw and red, echoing down the centre's polished corridors.

Watching the Teacher at his long table in the club I still wanted to know, and I figured I might find out too, because not long after he entered with his followers, his mam came in with the older brother, still wearing a face like thunder. I was expecting her to start her screaming again, but she didn't. It seemed like she'd changed tack and was going to try a different way to get to him.

Peter offered them seats at the table, but she refused.

'No love, no, it's Ok. You're with your friends. We'll be fine on our usual table, won't we Rhys? No, you stay here. But maybe we can have a little chat later is it? Just us?'

And then she went, taking Rhys with her to sit on another table up by the wall. The Teacher didn't bat an eyelid. Just let her go. Though he must have remembered her somehow, because of what he did later.

Garry had brought them all some sandwiches he was getting rid of from the bar. There weren't enough to go round so the Teacher split them between the whole table then, when they'd eaten them, he stood up and made a little speech. I couldn't hear what he said from where I was, but he spoke to all of them, and to each of them one by one. And whatever it was, it worked, because they all nodded and looked proper content when he was done. Before he sat down he made a toast, raising his glass and getting them all on their feet.

'Yesterday we were many,' he said. 'But today we are one. To Us!'

Then all the followers drank. But he didn't, at least not yet. Not until he'd raised his glass across the room to her too, to his mam. And not until she'd raised hers back. Then, and only then, did he drink from his.

It was after the raffle she finally got to him. I'd seen

her try twice before, getting up from her table clutching a photograph, only to be beaten by some-one else each time; someone else wanting to tell him their story. So she'd had to sit it out beside her other son, sit it out through the bands, the MC's jokes and the local opera singer belting out *Nessun Dorma*. But then the raffle came and she saw her chance.

Kev, the MC, had asked Peter to come and pull out the tickets. But Peter put the Teacher forward instead, shouting out as he made his way to the stage, 'It's alright Kev, I'll vouch for him!' releasing a groan across the whole room. It was as he was leaving the stage again that she caught him...

'Hello,' she said, all polite, like she was talking to a stranger. 'Do you remember me?'

'Yes,' he said. 'Of course I do. You're the woman from the shopping centre, aren't you?'

'Yes, I suppose I am.' She thought for a moment, then said 'Do you mind if I tell you a story?'

She must have seen how he couldn't get enough of people's stories, how he'd been devouring them ever since he'd arrived in town the day before.

'Is it your story?' he asked her.

'Well, it's more our story,' she said, a hint of hope lifting her voice. 'It's a story about us.'

She didn't give him a chance to ask any more, but just went straight on, making the most of this chink in his forgetting.

'You must have been, oh, I don't know. Eight? Nine maybe? Well, I'd been looking for you all over the house. It was late see, way past your bedtime, when I saw you out the window. And there you were, in the garden, on your own. Wearing your pyjamas you were. So I opened the window and shouted down to you. "What you doing there? I've been looking for you for ages! Stay there!" You remember that? Me shouting down to you? In my nightie? We still don't know how you got out there. The door was locked! You must have got out somehow though, because there you were, on your own in the garden. Me in my nightie shouting down at you.'

She paused then, looking for the ripples in his

expression she'd hoped her words might make. But there were none. Only that question again, the question he kept asking her, like torture.

'Who are you woman?'

I saw she wanted to scream at him again, but this was her one chance, so she held it in, held herself tight, laying a hand on his arm and speaking to him soft, low.

'I'm your mother, love. That's what I'm saying. Your mother. You don't remember? Me coming out to bring you back in? You didn't want to come at first. But you did in the end. You came inside, you came home with me. Come on love, let's go home is it?'

He shook his head. 'I can't. I'm with my friends. I can't leave them.'

She bit her lip, looking hard at him, as if her sadness was becoming anger. Then she pushed that photograph she'd been carrying into his hand.

'What about her? You remember her, don't you?'

He looked down at the photo. 'She's beautiful,' he said, still looking at it. 'Who is she?

'She's your daughter.'

And there it was. The ripple. She saw it, and so did I. A flicker of another man. A man who remembered. She grabbed his arm with her other hand too, holding on.

'That's your favourite photo of her. You remember that day. Down on the beach we were. She'd just come out the sea, all wet she was, and she came running up the beach calling at you, "Daddy, daddy!" And you picked her up, and you threw her in the air. And then I took this photo. As you were drying her off. You remember that? Look at her now. Look at her.'

And he did. Looked like I'd never seen someone look before. The whole club was still having a party, people getting back in their seats for the second half, the band warming up on stage, but he was somewhere else. He was on a beach again. A beach he remembered, drying a little girl he loved, a girl who was his daughter from a life he'd once lived.

When he lifted his head there was nothing but sadness in his eyes. Sadness and determination.

'Thank you,' he said, handing the photograph back to her. 'I have to go now.'

But she wasn't going to let him off that easy. 'No,' she said firmly. 'No, you keep it. You keep it now.'

And then it was her who left him. Left him standing there in the middle of the dance floor, staring down at that photo.

If Kev the MC hadn't drawn our attention to it, most of us would have missed what happened next. I'd gone back to the bar. Word had got round that The Band were on soon. Still here, still burning they were, and there was no way I was going to miss them for a second time that day.

Kev had come on to introduce them when his eye was caught by something else.

'Hey! Hey People! Look!' he said, pointing up at the wall behind me. 'Some bugger's left it record-ing!'

I turned round and saw he was pointing at the big screen, the one we watch Six Nations matches on. I took a step back to get a better view. It was the Teacher again, with Joanne. They'd gone into another room in the club and must have thought they were on their own. But they weren't, because a cameraman from one of the TV crews must have gone in before them, then set down his camera while he went off for a piss. So now there they were, the Teacher and Joanne, being broadcast to the whole club without their knowledge.

'Shhh,' Kev said, playing it for laughs. 'If we're quiet, maybe we'll see a bit of action!'

He needn't have shhh'd us because there was no sound on the feed. But we didn't need sound. At least I didn't, not to get an idea of what was happening in there.

The Teacher was asking her something. Again and again, explaining himself to her. But whatever it was Joanne was having none of it. She looked like she did on the slip the day before, when she was strapped with explosives. Scared, tearful, shaking and shaking her head. But the Teacher wouldn't let up. We saw him place his hands on her shoulders, saw her put her hand over her mouth, saw the tears come sliding down her cheeks. There'd been some laughing at first, but not now. The whole club was deadly quiet, watching this silent movie being played out before us.

Eventually he must have got through to her, because her shaking head became a nodding head. Yes, she seemed to be saying. I understand. I'll do this.

And then he kissed her. On the cheek, long and close, like a kiss of life. Or death.

Fair enough old Kev had a job on his hands to pick up the atmosphere when the two of them came back in again. He went straight for it though, firing off some jokes as they walked back to the table, stuff about 'slipping off for some private tutoring eh Teacher?' That kind of thing. But I could tell even Kev was shaken underneath, that even he was unsettled by what we'd seen.

But then The Band had come on and, well, everyone went wild for them, so I guess we forgot about it. Until what happened later that night. After which no one, not a single person who was in that club, would ever forget what they'd seen again.

As ever The Band didn't only make us go wild, but made ICU wild too, although in a very different way. They must have had their Company spies in the place because within minutes of The Band starting up one of their Resistance songs the whole party was raided, broken up by Old Growler and his wolf packs of Security.

This time The Band didn't get away, but were cuffed there and then on stage before being led out the back. As for the rest of us, it was just the usual stuff, photos taken, IDs checked, a few of the rowdier ones taken off for a beating in the back of a van. Old Growler was in his element, stalking the tables, eye-balling us all. He saved his special treatment for the Teacher though. Singling him out and making him stand up on the stage. We all waited for what he'd do to him next, but Growler, he was cleverer than that. He understood anticipation was the worst part of fear. So he did nothing. Just made the Teacher stand up there while he stared at him, stared at him good and hard like he was trying to kill him with looking.

After a while he knew he'd done enough. Rounding up his men, he ordered them out before giving the room one last scan of his own, then left us with one of his favourites.

'Enjoy your night,' he said to us all. 'It's your last.'

Then, turning to the Teacher.

'So make the most of it.'

I didn't fancy sticking around after that. No one knows how to execute a buzz kill quite like ICU, so to be honest I knew the night wasn't going to be rescued now Old Growler had done his business. So I left. As I was going though, passing the Teacher's table, I heard him lean across the back of a chair and speak to Joanne again. Now, I can't be sure, because the club was still loud and everything, the next band coming on stage, but this is what I think he said.

'If you're going to do it then do it now. Follow them.'

I carried on out the club doors but then stopped at the top of the stairs. Had he really just said that? Follow who? Old Growler's mob? And do what exactly? I was still trying to make sense of it when, sure enough, the club doors swung open and Joanne walked through them, then straight on down the stairs, head down, taking them fast, as if she had someone to catch up with, someone to catch.

I glanced back into the club through the windows in the door. The Teacher was up on his feet again, only this time he wasn't just up, but dancing too. Clapping his hands, swinging his arms and getting them all out on the dance floor, all his followers. Peter, the Legion Twins, Alfie, his brother, Simon, all of them rocking and shuffling out onto the dance floor to shake their stuff, with the Teacher leading them, shouting out to whoever'd listen,

'Let's dance! Let's dance!'

The next time I heard the Teacher he was shouting again, but unless I'd seen him myself, seen him with my own eyes, I'd never have thought that voice belonged to the same man.

He was crouching down on a piece of grass in the middle of the close where my girlfriend lives. I'd gone over to her house after the club because she hadn't been able to be there herself, so I wanted to tell her all about it. Her mam's been sick ever since she was twelve, so she spends most of her time caring for her and can't go out nights. We were sitting in her bedroom, talking, when I heard the shouting. I told my girl to stay put while I went to have a look, then went to the bathroom at the end of the corridor. Opening the window I looked down, and there he was. The Teacher, crouched on the grass, shouting and screaming.

A bunch of boys on bikes were cycling round and round him. Just kids they were, we all know them, annoying little shits causing trouble then wheelin' off. But nothing serious, nothing to shout about like he was doing down there. But shout he did. Again and again, cowering away from them as if they weren't kids at all, but demons.

I reckon he must have freaked them out in the end, because pretty soon they scarpered, leaving him alone whimpering on the grass. I looked to the head of the close. The club was just there, on the other side of the street. I could make out a bunch of people on the bench of the bus stop outside its car park. It was his followers. I could make out Alfie's bright jumper, and the Legion Twins, leaning against each other like one man leaning against a mirror. They were asleep, all of them. Nothing unusual in that. All of us have dozed off after a big night, haven't we? At the bus stop, in the train station. But the fact they hadn't been woken by the Teacher's shouting, well, that was weird.

I decided I'd go and wake them up. Tell them their man was having a bad trip or something. So I went and told my girl just that; that I'd be back in soon enough, but I had to go and sort out this bloke first, crouched on his own in the middle of the close. When I got out there though, he wasn't on his own. Old Growler was with him.

At least, I think it was Old Growler. It was hard to say. The close was dark and whoever the Teacher was talking to was wearing one of those Security gas masks. Only even that was different. The nose of it was longer, more like a snout. Like the snout of an animal. But the way the man stood, the way he did that little parade back and forth, the way he stabbed his finger in the air like his boss; all that made me think this was Growler, or at least some kind of a bad dream of him.

I couldn't hear what they were saying. The Teacher had stopped shouting now, and if he was speaking at all then it must have been softly. Bending double, I edged nearer, parking myself up behind one of the neighbour's garden hedges. I got there just in time to hear the end of their conversation.

'Tell me your story,' the Teacher said. Just as he'd said to everyone he'd met these past two days. 'Tell me your story.'

Silence. Just the sounds of the close sleeping, the tick of hallway clocks, the creak of a bedspring turning. I wanted to look, but didn't dare. I pressed my ear right into the hedge, straining to hear. And then, finally, he spoke.

'I have no story,' Growler said. 'I am.'

When I plucked up the courage to look over that hedge the Teacher was on his own again. Or was he? Again, it was hard to tell. There was no one else in the close now, but he was still talking. Looking up at one of the windows, talking, saying, 'I don't want to come in. I want to stay out here. I want to stay here.'

Then, all of a sudden he was down on his haunches again, his arms outstretched as if open to a child running towards him.

'Here you are!' he said as he stood up, throwing his arms in the air, catching a weight of nothing a moment later. 'Let's get you dry is it?'

I edged closer. He was on his knees, smiling, rubbing at the air with both hands. I followed the shape of them, the shape his hands made in the night and I saw it was a little girl. He was drying a little girl.

And then he wasn't.

Standing up again he turned to the head of the close. He'd seen someone else. Someone walking towards him, slow and steady. I could see his face clearly now, the one streetlamp catching his eyes. They were wet, filling with tears. Whoever was coming towards him must have been beautiful. I mean really beautiful. Because that's what his eyes said, that's what his face said, and that's what he said too, when she got to him.

'You look beautiful.'

Again I followed his hands, his arms, the way they embraced this person who wasn't there, and I saw this time it was a woman. A woman just a little shorter than him, her head resting against his shoulder as they began to dance. He held her so close, so tightly as they moved about that scrap of grass, I thought he'd never let her go. But then he did. Suddenly she was gone, and he looked just as surprised as me. He searched the air for where she'd just been, but it was of no use. He was alone again. As he sunk to his knees his head dropped and he pulled his hands through his hair, tearing at it in grief.

Right, I thought, I've got to help him now. Got to wake his brother or Peter, get them to take him to wherever he'd made his home. And I would have too, if only he hadn't spoken again, if only he hadn't spoken with that voice that wasn't his.

'That you son?' he said.

At first I thought he was talking to me. That somehow he'd seen me and was trying to scare me with this other voice, this deep, low voice, gentle but hard. But he wasn't talking to me, he was talking to himself.

'Dad?' he said in his usual voice.

He was looking up at one of the roofs now, as if he was speaking with someone up there.

'Hello son,' he said in the deep voice. 'You're out late.'

'So are you,' he replied, looking up to the roof again.

'You know me son,' the deep voice said again. 'Always working.'

And that's how it went. The Teacher standing on the grass in the middle of the close, looking up at one of the roofs, talking with himself. Talking as if he were two men, not one.

'Do you see me?' he said in his own voice.

'Of course I see you son,' replied the deep voice. 'I can see the whole town from up here. You should come up sometime. It's beautiful, especially at night.

If the moon's full it catches the terraces over on Western Avenue something lovely – makes it look like the street's made of silver. And all the lights in the windows too, turning on, turning off, each one telling a part of someone's story. You could set your watch by some of them. Mrs Evans, for instance. Over there on Brahms Road. Eight thirty every night her bedroom light goes off. I could count you down to it, it's that regular. Then Phil – you know Phil, don't you? Well, likes his reading does Phil. His light won't be off for another hour at least.

It's the same in the morning too. People do like their routines, don't they? There's one woman, over on Sandfields now, who walks the same way to work every day. Same way, same time, every day. Sometimes I want to throw something in front of her – piece of slate, one of my tools – just to make her go another way. Just once. But you can't, can you? Have to let people make their own choices. Isn't that right?'

'Yes,' the Teacher said in his own voice again. 'I suppose you do.'

'Can you see a piece of slate down there son?'

'A piece of slate?'

'Yes. It fell just now. Somewhere over there. Might not be much of it left. It's funny like that, slate. So strong, yet fragile in the end. No two pieces the same either, you know that? Might all look the same from down there, but I'm telling you, from up here you can see their differences. Different grain in each of them. That's the best way to work it too, you know that? Follow the grain – let the slate tell you where to go, what to do. Any luck?'

The Teacher looked down at his feet. 'No. Can't see it.'

'Try further over there,' he said to himself, using the deep voice again. 'By the path. Always a shame, isn't it? To see a shattered slate. All that work put into it, all that strength and grain, broken. Only way though, sometimes. Has to happen.'

'Does it? Why?' he asked himself as he walked over to the path.

'Well,' the deep voice explained. 'It's what people need sometimes, isn't it? Like a warning, a sign. Lets them know something's wrong with their roof. A roof, any roof now, is only as strong as its weakest slate see? One cracked slate, one loose one, that'll be where the water gets in. People always forget that. They'll look at the whole roof, from a distance like, and think "nothing wrong with that. Good roof that." But you got to get closer haven't you? Got to look at every slate. Listen to every slate. That's the only way to know for sure. But who does that? And no good telling them either. Usually a slate has to fall before they hear you. One has to fall, and then they'll listen. Shame, like I said, to lose a slate, but well, if it saves the whole house, got to be worth it in the long run, hasn't it?'

'I suppose so.'

He'd got to the path now and was looking down at it, as if he'd found something.

'What do you mean "you suppose so"?' he said in the deep voice again. 'What's one slate to a whole roof in the end? To a whole house? Small sacrifice I'd say. Now, have you found that piece yet?'

'Yes,' he answered quietly. 'It's broken.'

'Is it? Thought it might be,' said the deep voice. 'Never mind. Can you pass it up?'

Silence. For once he didn't answer himself, but just kept on looking down at the path.

'Son?' he said in the deep voice, soft and low. 'You going to pick it up?'

He looked up at the roof.

'Do I have to?' he asked.

'Yes,' he answered himself. 'I'm afraid you do son. Pick up the slate now. Pick it up.'

Moving very slowly the Teacher bent down to the path, picked something up, something dark and jagged, then stood again and held it in the air.

'Thank you, son,' he said in the deep voice.

Moving just as slow again, he dropped his arm. There was nothing in his hand.

'Well,' I heard him say in that low voice. 'I suspect you'll be on your way is it?'

'Yes.'

'Going on a journey are you?'

'Yes. I think so. Going on a journey.'

In the distance I could hear the grinding of a large

lorry, the lifting whine of a siren getting closer. The Teacher turned his head towards the street, towards the gathering sound.

'Well,' he said in the voice from the roof. 'I hope you've got everything you need. It's important to be ready, remember that son.'

'Yes,' he replied, his own voice sounding small in comparison, like the voice of a child. 'Thanks, Dad.'

And then he walked away. Walked away towards his sleeping followers and the sound of that lorry, grinding, and the sound of that siren, whining, both of them getting closer.

Book Three: Sunday

What I didn't know back then was that we all have different voices, just not all of us have found them yet. Because of what the Teacher did when he was here I've found one of mine, and I'm going to use it now to tell you what happened next. Why? Because to describe what happened that Sunday, to really describe it, would need a whole new language, let alone a whole new voice. But until we discover that language, this'll have to do.

If I'd known what the Teacher was walking towards that night, if I'd known the terrors waiting for him, I'd have run up that close and tried to stop him. But none of us knew, not then. Except him of course, I'm sure of it. That's why he wasn't surprised when he reached the end of the close and he saw Joanne standing on a wall, pointing at him.

'Thank you,' he said when she lowered her arm, sending a unit of Council police running over to him.

As they seized him, pulling his wrists behind him, gripping his shoulders, he managed to turn his head to look back. I followed his gaze to where it landed, right on the patch of grass where he'd danced with that beautiful woman of air; right where he'd danced with her, held her and lost her.

When he turned back again Sergeant Phillips was already reading him his rights, such as they were.

'I'm arresting you under the Public Disorder Act and the Insurgency Act, Emergency Amendment 14.2, making you subject to immediate preliminary trial.'

It was Sergeant Phillips and his barking that woke the Teacher's followers. When they saw the police holding him, the sergeant getting out his cuffs, they launched from that bus stop like a pack of dogs attacking a bear.

'Leave him alone!' the Teacher's younger brother

screamed. 'Get off him!'

'Sergeant Phillips, Sergeant Phillips!' Peter implored. 'I can vouch for him, I can. Come on now, leave him is it?'

Alfie and the Twins were the worst to witness. I suppose the Teacher had been the first person to see them, to hear them, for years. He was the man who just that same day had opened a door back to life for them, and now here he was being taken away. Alfie squirmed and beat like a wild animal against the grip of a constable, while the Twins howled and tore at another.

'Rest in peace!' they cried. 'Let him! Rest in Peace!'

'Go! Go Now!'

That was all the Teacher said to them. 'Alfie, Peter, boys. Go!'

And they did, ran for their lives into the night. And his mam and Rhys too. Only Peter stayed, still trying to negotiate with Sergeant Phillips.

But it was no good. The grinding lorry had already arrived, parking itself up in the social's car park.

That's where they took him, hoisting him up onto the flatbed, turning on the magnesium glare of two searchlights, making him squint and lower his head. A crowd had gathered now, drawn from the club and the houses in the close by the noise and the light. Which is, of course, just what they wanted. Nothing like an audience to get Old Growler going.

The Mayor opened proceedings, fumbling and mumbling over a set of prompt cards, a sharp-suited lawyer at his elbow. He said something about 'worrying reports', and rumours of a 'planned disturbance'. That 'in the interests of safety' and 'in the light of yesterday', the Council had been forced to take 'extraordinary measures', to prevent an imminent 'act of insurgency'.

He was way out of his depth. And anyway, everyone knew who was really running this show, so it was no surprise when Old Growler finally spoke, his voice carrying over the heads of the crowd from out the dark.

'What do you want?'

His voice was cold and clear. He knew he didn't

have to shout, at least not yet. He knew what scared us more than shouting; this voice like iced water, sharp and fluid, the accent of a bank manager from the mouth of a psychopath.

'Power? Respect? Is that it?'

He was standing on the cab of the lorry, his feet planted firmly on its roof, looking down at the Teacher. One of the searchlights swung up to catch him.

'Or are you doing this because everything else failed? Your job. Your marriage.'

He paused, waiting to see those words land in the Teacher. But they didn't. I'd come into the car park now, so I could see his face clearly. And there wasn't a flicker. He could have been standing down by that bus stop waiting for a bus, not on this flatbed being tried for his life. I saw that get Old Growler, and if there's one thing that bastard hated, it was being got.

'Oh, I know you,' he continued, pacing now, his steel-capped boots metallic on the lorry's cab. 'I know everything about you. Couldn't cope could you? So thought you'd pull that little stunt on the beach. Get yourself a band of merry men. Set yourself up as their "leader". I understand that. We're not so different you know.'

Again the Teacher didn't rise to it. Just stared at the ground below. In response to his silence Old Growler got louder.

'Because that's what they're saying, you know that? That you're going to lead them. You're going to make everything better. Is that what you told them? Is it?'

His voice echoed against the plastic and brick of the social, slid along the roofs of the houses.

'But what I want to know,' he carried on, getting all thoughtful. 'What I'd really love to know is on whose authority?'

He stopped pacing, looked down at the Teacher.

'Eh?' he said. 'Can you tell me that "Teacher"? Who elected you? Who voted for you? I'll tell you. Nobody!'

The crowd had grown. We were starting to sense it. This was bigger than ICU dealing with some troublemaker. This was bigger than Old Growler. This was bigger than all of us. And it didn't feel good, I can tell you. Like there was a chasm splitting through the town, cracking through the streets and gardens, heading straight for us and any minute now we were all going to fall right into it, right into the darkness.

I felt another light at the corner of my eye. When I turned I saw it was a camera's pack light. The TV crews were already here, getting their fill, sniffing through the audience for a bite. I heard the reporter approach someone behind me.

'Excuse me, sir,' he said. 'Can I have a word? For the camera. Are you an acquaintance of the accused?'

Another voice answered, low and quick.

'No. No I'm not.'

Up on the flatbed Old Growler was still at it.

'Or are you above Democracy? Some kind of a king are you? Is that it? Are you king of this town?'

He was shouting now. But sort of laughing too, like a hyena about to howl.

'Why so quiet? If that's what you've been saying in private, don't they deserve to hear it in public?

Come on, no need to be shy. Admit it! Or haven't you got the guts?'

The reporter was still at it behind me too.

'I'm sorry, but we saw you in the club. You were with the Teacher, weren't you?'

'I told you,' the other voice said. 'I don't know the man. Leave me alone.'

I knew that voice. I'd heard it tonight, just a few minutes ago. I turned round and there he was, staring up at the flatbed, his face tense with pain. Peter. Peter of the club, Peter the big friend of everyone, the go-to guy. There he was, denying all knowledge of ever having known the Teacher. He must have sensed it too; must have sensed where this was all heading. That if what the Teacher had been doing was threatening to get in the way of ICU and their plans, then the last place on earth you wanted to be was between them and him. And now I guess he wasn't. A few simple words, that's all it had taken. That's all betrayal is. A few letters put out on the air, as dangerous as the blade of a knife or a bullet in the chamber.

BOOK THREE: SUNDAY

Back on the flatbed Old Growler was really going for it now. There was something he needed, obviously. Something the Teacher would have to say before he could pounce. But the Teacher still wasn't giving it to him.

'Say it!' Growler was yelling down at him. 'You're the voice of these people! Their leader! Aren't you? Aren't you? Say it!'

But the Teacher wasn't saying anything. After all that talking with himself in the garden he'd gone mute. He just stood there in the glare of those lights, not looking down any more but up, up at the roof he'd been talking to before. Like he was listening, like someone else, someone more important than Old Growler, was also asking him a question.

And then suddenly, everything happened at once.

Growler was screaming now, all composure gone, while behind me the reporter was still pushing Peter, asking him again and again if he was a follower of the Teacher.

'Are you? Are you?' the reporter pressed.

'Are you? Say it! Are you?' Old Growler screamed.

'Are you?' they asked together.

From behind me, shouting at the top of his voice, Peter.

'I AM NOT!'

And then as if in answer, in distorted echo, the Teacher, breaking his silence like a whale breaking the surface of the sea.

'I AM!'

For a second the echoes of their cries were all that filled the night, the Teacher's eyes bright in the searchlights. But those words were what Growler had been waiting for. I saw a smile crack his face as he inhaled them before standing to his full height and jumping down onto the flatbed.

He landed with a two-booted thud.

'Thank you,' he said, striding up to the Teacher. 'Thank you. Now you're mine.'

Within minutes that car park was empty. The Teacher was swept down from the flatbed and into a Security van. The lorry's engine started, shaking its frame along the length of its chassis. The police and

ICU teams cleared the crowd.

Ducking under a uniformed arm, I ran back into my girlfriend's close, looking for Peter as I went. But there was no sign of him, no sign anywhere. Just as later, when I went for a piss in the middle of the night and I opened the bathroom window again, there was no sign of any of it. The Teacher on the grass, the bike boys, the woman and the girl made of air, the lorry, Growler's shouts, Peter's cry. All gone. The close was quiet, the car park empty and everything, everything in darkness.

In the morning I went running on the beach. I hadn't been running for years but I needed light and to feel my heart working, my lungs straining. More than anything though, I needed perspective and the morning air to clear my head.

When I got down to the front a sea mist was all the way in, so thick I couldn't see the water, Mumbles, the works. Everything was gone under white. But still I ran into it, and in a way it was perfect. Running blind into light. I found the wash of the waves then turned and ran with them on my left, running up towards the Naval to where this all began.

Flocks of knot waders were feeding in the shallows, scattered groups of them quick-stepping away from the waves. The seagulls above called like lasers from a sci-fi film and every now and then an early fisherman would ghost up out of the whiteness; a statue beside the tense question of his sea-tethered fishing rod.

It had all happened so quickly last night, too quickly. Suddenly I felt we'd all woken into a day we'd never asked for, a day when something was going to be spoiled forever. The Teacher had done nothing really, other than listen and be different. But it seems that was enough. Enough of a threat, and that such listening wasn't going to be allowed. Not when there were interests in the world whose currency depended on silence.

At the end of the dunes I turned round. What I saw looked like another beach. The sea mist had gone, blown off shore by a wind from the land. So I ran back into clarity, the hill above the town yellow-shot with gorse, the works ahead of me growing a plume of smoke like an *Ich Dien* feather on the Welsh rugby shirt. As I neared the town I saw a man sweeping his metal detector over the sands. Left, then right, left, then right, as regular as a metronome. In his other hand he trailed a spade. Someone else digging for riches. Well, if the stories doing the rounds the night before were anything to go by, he'd need something more powerful than that. From what I could tell ICU were definitely interested in some kind of valuable deposits under the town. Only thing was, they couldn't tell what they were; whether it was coal, minerals, gold. 'Geological interference' was the excuse their experts gave. But still they were sure it was valuable; apparently nothing could be that dense, that present, and not be. That's what the rumours said anyway.

As I ran the last bit of the beach up towards Franko's and Remo's I found myself thinking of a boy I'd once known. There was something in the look of the Teacher the night before, as he stood on the flatbed, that made me think of him. His name was Danny. I'd met him when I did a stint up at Hillside in Briton Ferry. A secure centre it is, for kids who get into trouble beyond the usual stuff. In my case, way beyond. It was a good place, run by good people. Sorted me out. But Danny had a hand in that, and that's why I found myself remembering him as I slowed to a walk and went to catch my breath down by the sea.

The whole time he was inside Danny worked every day on building a doll's house. He built it with quiet determination in the wood workshop, two hours every afternoon. We used to give him stick for it. As you can imagine, not the easiest place to throw yourself into building a doll's house, a secure centre for hard kids. But he did. Never broke his stride, however much he got teased or bullied over it.

He was following a book of instructions. Sometimes I'd catch him flicking through it, jumping ahead from where he was on the walls and roofs, to weeks down the line when he'd finally be building the beds, the window frames and maybe, if he did it in time, the people too.

Danny finished his doll's house a day before his release. When he went he didn't take it with him though but left it on the table in that workshop, perfectly painted, one half open to show the miniature world inside. We found it the next morning and when we did none of us said a thing. Suddenly it made sense, him building it like that. Him building what he didn't have but wanted, using his hunger to see him through. And then he'd left it behind, to show us what we didn't have, but what we could have, if we aspired to it.

And that, I thought, as I took the steps back up onto the prom, was what the Teacher had been doing here. At least, that's what I reckoned at the time. He'd arrived on this beach two days ago with no story, no memory. So he'd gone and found some and in doing so he'd showed us to ourselves. Like Danny he'd used his hunger to make us remember. And that's why, as I walked through Sandfields on my way home, I decided to follow him that day, follow him to the end of whatever he'd come to do here.

The Company Man wanted it all out in the open. That much was clear as soon as I got to the civic centre. No behind-the-doors tribunals. No private courts. Under the contract ICU had signed with the town five years ago any criminal activity threatening Company interests could be decreed an internal matter, subjecting the accused to Company adjudication and disciplinary measures. I can trot that out because I've heard it read to me in a windowless room more than once. So I know what those 'disciplinary measures' can be; we all do. Now. A lesson in reading the fine print if ever there was one. But, like I said, this time the Company Man had decided to make it a public affair. A public trial. After all, weren't the media easier to control than rumour?

As I'd come through town I'd seen even more families thrown out of their homes. A big group of them had set up camp opposite the police station. Maybe that's just where they'd ended up; I don't know. Or maybe they'd gone there because they'd heard that's where the Teacher was being held. Either way I couldn't see it helping his case. Just more ammunition for ICU, another reason to get rid of him.

But I'd forgotten what a slick operator the Company Man could be. I was being too crude in my thinking. That would have been too easy, predictable; just to charge the Teacher, try him and disappear him. And that wasn't what this was about anymore. It wasn't a case of just getting rid of him. No, it was more about proving him wrong, about obliterating not just the man himself, but the idea of him.

There was a massive crowd. The whole civic area was packed. Whether they'd been forced to come or had just come to see the show, I couldn't tell. What I did know was that, like me, some were there for him. Some were there just to witness him follow this through. What none of us were expecting though was for two hooded prisoners, not one, to be led from the police van when it sirened into the centre of the square and opened its doors.

They made the two of them stand up on the stage in the centre of the area; each facing away from the other, both of them still hooded. And that's how they remained as the Company Man's voice suddenly spoke to us, strong and firm over the tannoy, his face lighting up on the big screen behind us.

'Good afternoon everyone. It's good to see you all.'

Then there he was, striding out onto the stage as polished and deadly as ever, his purple tie flicking its tail in the breeze.

'When I spoke to you here two days ago,' the Company Man continued, speaking into a lapel mike, leaving his hands free to gesture with reason-ableness. 'I warned you that the enemies of progress were still working among us. Sadly, as we have all witnessed over the last few days, those same enemies have taken advantage of what is a delicate time of transition for this town and used it to try to meet their own selfish ends.'

He paused, standing between the two hooded men. He was in his element. In control once more. Granting us one of his slow gazes over the crowd he was about to continue when something stalled him. I saw it in his eyes; something was out of place, wrong. It was the same way I'd seen him look on the beach two days ago, and when I followed his eyes, it was for the same reason too. They were back. The two women and the little girl, still wearing their nightclothes, standing in a line at the far edge of the crowd, still watching.

The Company Man cleared his throat, playing for time, adjusted his tie then carried on, fuelling his speech by striding towards the first hooded man.

'Standing before you today,' he said as he went. 'Are two of those selfsame enemies.'

Reaching the man, he pulled off his hood. A gasp travelled through the crowd. It was Barry Absolem. We all knew him. His mam had run one of the clubs before it was closed down. A few months later she'd closed herself down too. It was Barry who'd found her, half out her bed, the bottle of pills empty on the pillow beside her.

'One,' the Company Man declared, pointing to Barry. 'A would-be assassin and terrorist who thinks nothing of killing his own kind to achieve his aims.'

Barry had been the bomber. It was his voice we'd

all heard that day. The Company Man let this sink in for a moment before striding over to the second man.

'The other,' he said, removing his hood with a flourish. 'Is a man who would tear down the very fabric of our society, and who is an affront to every-thing that we hold dear.'

The Teacher didn't flinch. Didn't catch his eye or anyone else's. He just stood there, as if alone.

'Now, ladies and gentlemen,' the Company Man continued, turning his back on the Teacher. 'As you can see, I have decided to make this adjudica-tion public. That is why I have invited you here. That is why I have invited these cameras. Because I want to show you that we at ICU have nothing to hide. I want you to witness. I want you to witness the arguments of these men. This town is rife with rumour. With stories. I understand that such rumours spread fastest and furthest when people feel they are being kept from the truth. So today I want to show you the truth.'

He paused, as if expecting the word to trigger us

again; here, in the same place where just two days earlier a young woman had been shot as she shouted out that same word. But no one shouted now. No one started a chant. He'd caught us all off guard, and he knew it.

Allowing himself the slightest of smiles he moved on again, pacing around the stage.

'One of these men,' he said as he walked. 'Says that over the five years we've been working here, we have given the town no choice. The other man says personal choice is all that matters. He wants us to live in a different way. Without families, without work. Without homes. Everything should be shared, nothing owned. Well, today I am going to give *you* a choice. Because at the end of this trial, one of these men shall walk free. And the choice as to which man walks will be yours.'

Spinning on his heel he turned to face Barry. 'Name?'

Barry's head had been hung low but he lifted it now, showing us all the black swelling of a bruise shutting one of his eyes.

'Barry,' he said. 'Barry Absolem.'

The Company Man pointed at him. 'Were you,' he asked, 'the bomber behind the assassination attempt on Friday?'

Barry turned to look at him. 'It wasn't a...'

'Answer the question!'

'Yes,' Barry said, turning away. 'Yes I was.'

'And what is your argument, Barry?' The Company Man turned to us now, to the crowd, opening his arms. 'You may speak to the people.'

We all looked at Barry. Was he really giving him a chance? Was there really a possibility ICU would let a bomber go free over a Teacher? A man who'd done nothing but forget, listen and help us remember? Barry obviously didn't think so. If he had, perhaps he'd have tried to defend his actions. As it was, he just explained them.

'Well, it's not right, is it?' he said looking straight back at the Company Man. 'You say you're here to help us, but you don't. You use us. You deal in mineral prices, share prices, markets. Everything about us, here, is decided elsewhere. It's all about the Company men now, not the working men. We're just a product to you, a product with a sell-by date. And when that date comes, you'll just get rid of us all together.'

He turned to us now, to the crowd. 'But we're not a product, we're people. And people don't have a sell-by date.'

The Company Man laughed. Perhaps he didn't mean to, but he did. 'I think you'll find they do, Barry,' he said. 'It's called death.'

But Barry wasn't going to let a cheap joke take away his point. 'Not if they're a town,' he said, his voice choking in his throat. 'A town never has to die.'

The Company Man shot him a look. As if he realised he couldn't play this one by halves. Pointing at him again, he strode back towards him.

'You strapped an innocent woman with explosives. Then made her walk into a crowd of men, women and children!'

'But I didn't detonate them, did I? You will. When the time comes you'll press the button on this town. You already have! Look at all the people thrown out of their homes!'

The Company Man jumped on that one. 'They will be given new homes.'

'But it should be their choice!'

A murmur of approval ran through the crowd. The Company Man sensed it. Knew if he was going to go for the kill, then the time was now.

'You want to know about choice, Barry?' he said, narrowing his eyes and getting in close to his face. 'There are easy choices and hard choices. The fact is that we make the hard choices for this town. The difficult choices people would rather not make for themselves. As for the easy choices, well they seem to like the choices we give them. The subsidised food. The free Xboxes in Company homes. The Company fuel tokens and cars. If they really cared about what you're saying wouldn't they speak through the choices they make, Barry? You don't want to defend their choices, Barry. You just want to defend the past, that's all.'

Holding the silence after his last word for a second he quickly spun away from him and paced to the other side of the stage. If Barry had an answer to that, he wasn't going to hear it. He'd had his chance, slim though it was. And now it was gone.

'Name?' the Company Man asked walking up to the Teacher.

'I don't know.' His voice was calm, as if someone had asked him the time.

'They call you the Teacher.'

'If you say so.'

The Company Man nodded, as if taking the temperature of his answer, weighting how to play this. 'You have been charged with leading a revolt against the Council and the Company,' he said, strolling away from him. 'And of planning insurrectionist activities. Is this true?'

'If you say it is.'

Another intake of breath from the crowd. Why did he say that? We all knew it wasn't true. The Company Man was filling the Teacher with his own fears. He turned to look at the Teacher again, obviously as surprised as us.

'What is your argument Teacher?'

'I have no argument.'

Again the Company Man looked wrong-footed. He'd prepared his debate, his points. But how was he meant to execute them if this man wouldn't defend himself?

'Alright,' he said. 'Then I'll tell the people your argument.'

Walking to the front of the stage he addressed us, his eyes flicking for just a second to those two women and the little girl in their nightdresses.

'You believe,' he said, pointing at the Teacher. 'In the breakdown of society. In tearing up the social contract. You say that everyone is of the same value, regardless of their contribution. You don't recognise the family unit, the importance of work, of money, or economic wealth. You say little to your followers, but expect them to give up everything. Is that right?'

The Company Man was good. He didn't sound as if he was accusing the Teacher, more trying to understand him. But he was clever too. He was framing what the Teacher was and while his words made sense there, up on stage, we knew they bore no relation to what had happened over the last two days on the streets, in people's houses, on the mountain.

'If you say so,' the Teacher replied again.

'Why did you come here?' the Company Man asked. His tone was different. The question was real, instinctive. He really wanted to know. 'Why did you come back?'

At last, the Teacher turned to face him. 'To listen to the truth,' he said.

And there it was. A word he could grasp at, a word he could use to engage his argument. 'But whose truth?' he asked. 'What truth? It's like what I said to Barry. You're ignoring the fact that we, the Company, deal with the hard truths. The unpalatable truth. If these people want a certain way of life, then certain compromises have to be reached. You know that. We deal with the truths ordinary people don't want to even look at!'

He addressed us again. 'Where is your power going to come from tonight? How will you call your cousin, hundreds of miles away? How will you afford your weekly shop? How will you keep warm in the winter? It's the truths of these questions that we deal with, Teacher.'

Extending his arm he pointed directly at his face. 'Are those the truths you came to hear?'

'No.'

'At least he's fighting to protect something,' the Company Man continued, gesturing to Barry now. 'To protect the town he knows. You, you're more dangerous than that. You're not protecting anything. You just want to break everything up.'

The revelation in his voice seemed genuine. As if it was only now, standing opposite him, that the Company Man really understood the threat the Teacher posed.

'But you need him, don't you?' the Teacher said. 'And he needs you.'

The Company Man stared at him, incredulous. 'Why would I need him?'

'Because he challenges you, and that justifies what you do.'

'And you don't challenge me?'

'No. I make you unnecessary.'

It was like a punch to his stomach. I swear, I saw the blood drain from his face there and then. He went to answer, but for once he was lost for words.

'I see you,' the Teacher said. 'I know your story.'

Silence. The whole civic centre tensed with anticipation.

'And what,' the Company Man said, half swallowing his words. 'Might that be?'

The Teacher returned his gaze, calm and steady. 'You are afraid.'

The Company Man looked down at his feet and took a deep breath. Everyone will say different but for me that's when the dice were rolled. That's when the choice was made. I saw it in his eyes when he raised his head and looked at the Teacher again.

'Am I?' he said. 'Well, let's see. Let's play this by your rules, shall we? I want to give the people of this town a choice today. But not by a vote. Everyone knows a vote can be rigged. And that's what you'd say, isn't it? That I loaded the crowd. So how would you do this? Maybe by giving the choice to just one person? One innocent person. Because everyone's choice is as valid as anyone else's, isn't it?'

Turning to the crowd he scanned the front rows, a twitching smile at the corner of his lips. He had a plan; I could tell, and I didn't like the look of it.

'You,' he said, pointing to someone in the crowd. 'You, the girl in the blue jumper. Can we get her up here please?'

I turned to the big screen, saw the camera run along faces until it landed on a little girl. She couldn't have been more than seven or eight. Then some hands came in and picked her up. I looked back to the stage just in time to see Old Growler carry her up the steps and put her down in front of the Company Man.

'Hello,' he said, kneeling down to her height. 'What's your name?'

'Katy,' she said, her voice carrying on his lapel mike. She was wearing an oversized blue hoodie, the sleeves rolled up to show her small hands. I'd seen it somewhere before, but I couldn't think where.

'Well, Katy,' the Company Man continued, one hand on her shoulder to reassure her. 'I don't want you to be nervous. I'm just going to ask you three questions, is that alright?'

She nodded.

'Just answer as truthfully as you can. Can you do that for me?'

She nodded again.

'Ok. Well, let's start,' he said as if about to read her a bedtime story. 'Katy, do you want to carry on living with your family?'

'Yes,' she said, her voice small and clear.

'Of course you do. And do you want to live with them in your house? In your home?'

'Yes,' she said again, nodding. I looked at the hoodie, racking my brain where I'd seen it before. And then I remembered. On the beach, that morning, when the Stranger had dressed him. It was the hoodie the young lad had given him. And then again, right here, when the woman was shot. The Teacher had taken it off and lain it over her. It was his hoodie, on this girl. Suddenly, knowing that, I felt better. Perhaps, just maybe, the Company Man wasn't pulling the strings on this one after all?

'Last question Katy,' he said, giving her a warm smile. 'And in that house, would you like to keep all your toys, your TV, your games?'

She paused, thinking for a moment. But we all knew what was coming. The poor girl was just that, a little girl, and these question were ridiculous. Ridiculous and yet terrifying. 'Yes,' she said eventually, returning his smile.

'Thank you Katy,' the Company Man said. 'Thank you very much.' He stood up, giving her a pat on the head. 'A big hand for Katy everyone!'

As she was taken back down the steps the Company Man took a deep breath as if to say, 'that was a close one, but now we're back on track.' He looked out over the crowd.

'The verdict has been delivered,' he announced. 'And it is a good verdict. The freed man might be reckless, dangerous even. He is certainly outdated, but at least he is fighting to protect what you have here. At least he is trying, in his way, to keep things together.'

Without looking at him he pointed to Barry.

'Free him.' Immediately Old Growler's men went to him, removing his cuffs. Barry looked down at his wrists trying to comprehend what was happening.

'This one,' the Company Man continued, pointing with his other hand, arm outstretched, to the Teacher. 'He's yours.'

Then he turned to look at him. The Teacher returned his gaze as the Company Man spoke again. 'Make an example of him,' he said. 'In the old way.'

As soon as he spoke word became deed. Before the Company Man had even turned away Old Growler's pack dogs were on the Teacher, sweeping him off the stage in a black swarm of body armour, helmets and gloves. Maybe the Company Man hadn't known which of the two men would be charged that day, but Old Growler, he'd always known who he wanted. And now he had him.

They dragged him through the crowd and into the shopping centre. The camera followed but it was no use; he was gone. Someone else though suddenly found it. A pair of hands grabbing the lens and swinging the image towards their face.

'I know him! I can vouch for him! I'm his follower!'

It was Peter, shouting into the lens, crying, screaming what he hadn't said just twelve hours earlier. But no one wanted to listen. Not even Growler's men.

'I am!' Peter cried, as the screen went blank and he was swallowed by the crowd. 'I am!'

When the screen flickered into life again it took a few seconds before we realised what it was showing. The images were coming from inside the shopping centre now, taken on a camera phone. But this was no accident, no leak. They wanted us to see this. They wanted us to watch as Growler's men went to play on the Teacher's head, body and face. As they tore his skin with the soles of their boots. As they broke his bones with their fists and their knees. As they showed him who he was to them. Which was nothing, nothing.

And then we heard it too. The Teacher's screams,

echoing down those empty corridors, between those silent shop-window dummies, their blank faces looking on as he got free of their hold, staggered away, slipping on his own blood, only to be caught again and beaten again under the cheerful smiles of holiday posters.

It was all too much, too much. Where had this come from? Behind me I could hear the screams of his mam as her other sons dragged her away. The cries of the Legion Twins, rocking and rocking behind me as they discovered the beautiful world he'd given them could be darker, more cruel than anything they'd ever known before.

And it was too much for Sergeant Phillips too. After a minute of that footage up on the screen he broke ranks and ran towards the cordon of ICU security guarding the entrance.

'Let me in!' he bellowed at them. 'Let me in! This is my town, my jurisdiction!'

But it was too late. Everything was too late.

Shortly afterwards one of Growler's men came out, clipped off a run of barbed wire, then went back in. None of us wanted to know what they were going to do with it, but it was the barbed wire that really told us, when they finally emerged again bringing the ravaged Teacher with them, what this had all been about. Power and fear.

They'd crowned him with it. Someone in there, no doubt Old Growler himself, had taken the time to weave that wire into a crown, then push it onto the Teacher's head, so hard the barbs scraped against his bone.

'Your king!' Growler shouted to us as he held up the Teacher by the scruff of the neck. 'The king of your town!'

Shoving him before him he began to walking back to the police van. 'You!' he shouted to Sergeant Phillips. 'Bring your men. Follow me!'

He turned away again and walked three or four metres before he realised Sergeant Phillips hadn't moved. 'I said,' he shouted back to him. 'Follow me!'

Sergeant Phillips stood taller. Old Growler passed the Teacher to one of his pack dogs, then strode back to face up to Phillips. 'That,' he said, 'was an order.'

Sergeant Phillips stared down at him. Then, slowly, he lifted his hand to his head, removed his beret and threw it to the floor. Old Growler looked at it, then looked at the rest of Phillips' men. One by one they all did the same, until there was a litter of berets at their feet, like dark petals shed across the civic centre's floor.

Growler didn't wait to see anything else. Turning on his heel he strode back to the van, hit it twice on the side, and then they were gone. They had taken him.

You'll hear all sorts of stories about what happened next. But so few people were there it's hard to know which are true. So I'll just tell you what I heard, what people were saying in the days and weeks after, about what they did to him.

About how they'd taken him to the stonemason's yard up by the road to watch his own gravestone being carved.

How the mason had asked him his name and when he hadn't answered how Old Growler had said 'he's forgotten,' and how that's what the mason carved – FORGOTTEN.

How they made him a new crown, from brambles this time, and how they pushed its thorns into the wounds made by the first.

About how they'd made him carry his own cross from there to the front. About how Old Growler had said, 'History, wasn't it? What you taught? You should enjoy this.'

About how when he fell strangers came to help him.

How the Company Man had watched him stagger back into the civic centre, bent double under the weight, splinters in his back.

How he'd seen enough, so left with Growler and the rest to take up their front-view seats for the show.

How when he entered the shopping centre, everything changed.

BOOK THREE: SUNDAY

The women of the town had made it theirs.

When Growler had taken him, they'd come. No one had called them, they'd just arrived, from streets and houses all over town. And after they did, they'd begun cleaning; washing his blood from the walls and the floors. And then they'd waited.

When he got to them he was broken. Bleeding from every limb, blinded by his own blood. His mam was there, and she led the women in the washing of his body. My girl was there too, and it was her who told me this. How they kneeled in a circle, passing the white towels from the bucket of water to his mam, then back to the bucket.

How that water turned from clear to pink to red.

How his mam couldn't remove the crown of brambles, so she wove it instead; wove it with red flowers to hide his blood.

How the sound of the water running from the towels into the buckets was like bells, and how he never asked his mam, 'Who are you?' again, because he knew now, not from memory, but from what she was doing for him.

How she dressed him in that blue hoodie again and how when she bent low to listen to his whisper all he'd said was, 'Look how I make the world new.'

And how that was enough.

By the time he reached the roundabout the light was already dying from the day. A crowd had gathered again, but was so quiet I could hear the fall of the waves down on the beach and the creaking of the ICU dignitaries' chairs up on the balcony of the Four Winds.

They'd built a platform for his cross. Made out of doors it was, all the doors that they'd taken in the last few days.

When they laid him on it I couldn't see him any more. But I heard the nails being hammered in. Tap. Tap, tap. Tap. Tap, tap.

ONE.
TWO.
THREE.

He screamed. And when he did, it carried to the mountain I swear.

Then suddenly, there he was again, rising over the heads of the crowd. They'd stripped him so I could see his chest working quick and shallow, trying to keep the breath in his lungs. For a moment that was the only new sound; his breathing, falling between the turning of the waves. But then he began screaming again; long cries of pain, alone up there, screaming and screaming.

And then a voice started singing. A male voice, strong and proud. And as it sang, so his screams subsided, until he was screaming no more.

It was his younger brother. The sad one from the slip who'd joined him. He was standing at the foot of the cross, looking up at the Teacher, not singing him to sleep, but to death.

'Cariwch', medd Dafydd, 'fy nhelyn i mi,
Ceisiaf cyn marw roi tôn arni hi.
Codwch fy nwylo i gyraedd y tant;
Duw a'ch bendithio fy ngweddw a'm plant.'

And then the Teacher spoke. At first I couldn't hear what he said, but then he said it again. And again.

'I remember. I remember.'

And then it happened. Still no one you talk to here will tell you how, or even exactly what. But what they will say is that was the moment, that was when we were saved.

It began with a low rumble. Like thunder several valleys away. Then the rumble became a sensation, a shiver under our feet. And all the time the Teacher up there saying, 'I remember, I remember.'

The rumble got louder and as it did the first few planks of the platform broke off and fell to the ground. And it was then, too, that he raised his voice, and told us.

'I remember,' he cried, 'Beech Hill! The Trafalgar Ball! The beach wreck! Tump number 9! The Majestic! The Regent! The Palace! Egan's! Players! Bernies! The Forge Road Baths! The Starlight Club! Harvey's Lake!'

And he went on. Like a torrent it was, a flow of the gone town pouring from his mouth. Everything that had been taken, back. And as he spoke, so they came out of the ground from under him. What, you ask? Well, good question. How to tell you? I suppose the most simple way to put it is us. Us, we came out of the ground. Our memories, our parents' memories, their parents' memories. And with them our stories. Everything that made us, everything that made the town more than just bricks and glass and concrete.

It was like my bampa said, wasn't it? Cleverest thing the Company ever did, to make us forget where we came from so as to make us blind to where we were going. Well, right then, as the sun sank over Swansea, as the wet sand on the beach turned the colours of an oyster shell, he made us remember. And in doing so, made us see.

But he could only hold on for so long. Soon the words were slowing, his voice getting quieter. And with it all those images and sounds coming out of the ground began to die down too. Until eventually they were gone.

And so was he.

In the silence that followed I don't think anyone even breathed. We'd all, as one, been taken somewhere, and then suddenly we were back. Back, but different.

I looked up to the balcony of the Four Winds to where the Company Man had been watching with his lackeys from the Council. Then others turned to look at him too, until the whole crowd was staring at him, daring him to speak.

When he did, it was with the voice of a beaten man. He knew he'd done this to himself. In killing the Teacher he'd showed everyone what the wealth under this town was.

'If that's what matters to you,' he finally called out, trying to muster some pride, 'then there's nothing of value here for us. We won't be back.'

With a sweep of his arm he took them all off that balcony with him, disappearing out the back and into their cars. Old Growler didn't need any other order. Calling his men to him he left too, quick marching them down the slip and out into the darkness of the beach and their waiting boats.

And then we were alone.

No one said anything. They just came forward and did what they had to. Both his brothers, Sergeant Phillips, Alfie, the Legion Twins. Hoisting two white sails up and over the cross they wound them round his chest as Sergeant Phillips and Rhys hammered out the nails from his hands and feet. Then they lowered him, lowered him like a flag, his body loose and heavy, into the lap of his mother.

For a moment she held him there, her son who'd forgotten her, then known her better than ever. As Joanne and Simon brought a shroud to cover him she sang, just as if she was singing him to sleep as a baby.

'So sleep on now, come take your rest
The hour is soon to come.
Behold us now, for it is night
We'll rise again at dawn.
And sleep.
And sleep.

And sleep.'

As she came to the end of her song Joanne began to pull back the shroud. She was right, we all wanted to see him one last time. His mam nodded, lifting her hand to stroke his hair. But when the shroud dropped away, he wasn't there.

He'd gone. And in his place were flowers. Like someone had planted a spring meadow inside him and now, with his death, it had taken bloom. Joanne kept pulling back the shroud, and they kept falling out, a waterfall of flowers, as fresh as if just picked.

We all must have been staring at those flowers because the first I knew of Uncle Bryn standing up on the platform was when he hit his staff against it.

'Bang,' it went, and we all looked up to see him standing there, his big puppet-master's hood half over his face.

He hit the platform twice more, quick and sharp.

'Bang, bang.' And then he spoke, loud and booming, as if calling to someone on the mountain.

'It is finished!'

Ever the showman he followed his voice with a big sweeping bow, so when he stood up again that hood came falling off his head onto his shoulders.

And there he was, I swear. The Teacher. Bold as brass.

He looked over us all staring up at him, and then he spoke to us.

'It has begun!' he said.

And then he was gone.

So that's what happened. And that's how it happened. Here, to us. Someone else will probably tell you different but like I said, I know what I saw and I know what I remember. And I know he was here and then he wasn't. And I know how we are now, well, it's different to how we were before. And if it wasn't for the Teacher then that wouldn't be the case.

Believe me.

Acknowledgements

The Gospel of Us was first commissioned and published as a limited edition of 1000 by NTW as part of its thirteenth production: *The Passion*, April 2011, Port Talbot. Many thanks to Lucy for speed-reading the first draft, Adele Thomas for all her work on the ground, Weird Naked Indian for providing the anthem for the performance *Home is Where the Heart is*, Taibach Rugby Club, the Naval Social Club, the cast and crew of *The Passion* and all the people of Port Talbot.

Weird Naked Indian, *Home is Where the Heart is*
http://nationaltheatrewales.org/sites/default/files/HomeIsWhereTheHeartIs.m4a

www.port-talbot.com

By the same author:

Poetry
The Blue Book
Skirrid Hill
A Poet's Guide to Britain (Ed.)

Fiction
Resistance
White Ravens

Non-fiction
The Dust Diaries

Screenplay
Resistance (with Amit Gupta)

Plays
The Passion
The Two Worlds of Charlie F.